ALAN C. WILLIAMS

FIRESTORM

Complete and Unabridged

LINFORD
Leicester

First published in Great Britain in 2019

First Linford Edition
published 2020

A catalogue record for this book is available
from the British Library.

ISBN 978–1–4448–4576–1

Published by
Ulverscroft Limited
Anstey, Leicestershire

Set by Words & Graphics Ltd.
Anstey, Leicestershire
Printed and bound in Great Britain by
T. J. International Ltd., Padstow, Cornwall

This book is printed on acid-free paper

FIRESTORM

1973: Debra Winters has started a new life for herself as a teacher in a small Australian outback town. Given the responsibility of updating the school's fire protocol, she is thrown together with volunteer firefighter Robbie Sanderson, and there's a spark of attraction between them. Meanwhile, things are heating up: it's bushfire season, and there's an arsonist on the loose. Debra and Robbie find themselves in danger. Will their relationship flicker out — or will they set each other's worlds alight?

1

Sprinting over the playground caused a few heads of the milling students to turn. They'd probably never seen a teacher run; another first for this new girl. Technically I was a woman but I still felt like an active teenager, physically at least.

'Hello, Miss Winters,' a few of them called out.

'G'day girls,' I replied, stopping at the door of the main building to pull off my sandshoes and slip on low heels over my panty hose.

A quick adjustment of my blouse and skirt and I was ready to face the critical eye of my headmaster, Ken-call-me-Kenneth Lawson.

'Morning ladies,' I greeted Mrs. Bennett and Mrs Alliprandi as I walked briskly past. The school secretaries both glanced pointedly at their watches, tutting. My first week at All Saints was

1

shaping up to be my last.

The staff room door was closed and I heard Mr Lawson's dulcet tones from the other side. Without pausing, I opened the heavy door and walked into the morning staff briefing. Peering at the assembled nine teachers at our school, I gave them my biggest and warmest smile before saying, 'Traffic was murder.'

No one laughed. The fact that I'd seen less than a dozen cars in the last thirty miles in my drive from Hobart meant my excuse was a joke.

'You're late, Miss Winters,' said Mr Lawson in his sternest Headmaster voice.

'Actually, I'm not, Mr Lawson, sir. The briefing is at quarter to nine and that's . . . ' I pointed to the clock on the wall over the notice board, 'still two minutes away.' I gave him a wide grin. 'Debra Winters versus Kenny Lawson — fifteen-love.'

Principal Lawson glanced at his watch then at the staff-room clock, comparing the times. I wondered if he'd realised that the clock had been set back a few minutes by yours truly yesterday arvo before I'd gone home.

Semper paratis was the boy scout motto and it was mine too. Turning clocks back had worked on Mum when I was in school, enabling me to grab some extra telly time or reading my teen newspaper *GoSet*.

'Hmm,' Mr Lawson acknowledged. I gave Doris a wink as he quickly reviewed what I'd missed. It was effectively nothing. The usual warnings about the length of girls' skirts, boys making sure their shirts were tucked in and ties tied and, just in case everyone had forgotten from yesterday's identical briefing, any jewellery, make-up and nail polish was to be removed in Roll-Call.

Mr Lawson was a firm believer of setting and maintaining standards. He seemingly abhorred progress, only grudgingly conceding that Australia's change over to the Metric system would make teaching distances and weights easier.

He was paranoid that the permissive Sixties that had ruined Mother England and large cities in Australia might finally began to seep into our own island paradise of Tasmania. As Bob Dylan had said, *The Times Were a-Changing*. Pity Mr Lawson didn't accept that.

'We must remember that we at All Saints have high standards to maintain. Repeat the school motto after me: All Saints High School. We always set our standards high.'

Like a bunch of sleepy parrots, the staff repeated our motto. There was little enthusiasm apart from me. We turned to our staff-room desks, already piled high with papers and text books but Mr Lawson wasn't finished.

'I almost forgot ... with all the bushfires over in the Derwent Valley and the Midlands, I've asked the chief of the Huonville volunteer firefighters to visit each of our classes today to brief the students on common-sense safety precautions. We've had an early spring meaning lots of plant growth, followed

4

by four months of dry summer heat. The hills around here are tinder-dry. It's only a matter of time before we have fires nearby.'

I piped up. 'There was a fire up at Mountain River yesterday. I saw the smoke going home.'

'Quite so, Miss Winters. You should all expect to see Mr Sanderson this afternoon in class.'

Our art teacher, Mr Morris, looked up from his crossword. 'Sanderson? Not Robbie Sanderson?'

Mr Lawson consulted his page-a-day diary. 'Robbie? Why yes. Is that a problem, Mr Morris?'

Scanning the faces of many of my colleagues, Archie Morris wasn't the only one who seemed put out. The intrigues of country towns. I wondered if I'd done the wrong thing coming here. It had been a last-minute decision, necessitated by a disaster in my personal life. All Saints was the only school with a vacancy for an English teacher and right now, I could see why.

The headmaster continued, 'I'm aware that All Saints fire procedures are sadly out of date. Could we have a volunteer to review them?'

No one responded. A few examined their fingernails or stared out of the window towards the distant Huon River or, in Archie's case, at his crossword.

'We should have a fire evacuation drill too, Mr Lawson,' I stupidly suggested.

'Ah. Our volunteer. Fire protocol update plus practice run for evacuation. Thank you so much, Miss Winters.'

Damn! Why couldn't I keep my mouth shut?

'But . . . but I don't know the school at all. I've only been here three days.'

It was true. The school year in Australia started late January or early February, in the midst of our summer. Bushfires were a problem this time of the year. Being stitched up with an admin job so quickly after beginning teaching here was uncalled for. Mr Lawson wasn't backing down, though.

'Then it will be an exceptional opportunity to learn about our little outpost of education, Miss Winters. Thanks for volunteering. Shall we say a week? I await your proposals with bated breath.'

It wasn't fair. Fortunately for me, our American maths teacher came to my aid.

'I'll help out, Debra. Catch up during free period before lunch?'

'Thanks, Doris,' I replied. Doris de Shannon looked so much like Lucille Ball from *I Love Lucy*, I wondered if they were twins. She was the only teacher here who had tried to befriend me.

Mr Lawson clapped his hands.

'Right, everyone. Time for Roll-Call. Not you, Miss Winters . . . a quick chat, if you please. Mrs Jones will take 3A for Roll-Call, won't you?'

Mrs Jones nodded, picked up her walking stick and hobbled out. All but three of us were in their late fifties or older. No wonder All Saints was struggling to maintain student numbers.

The assemblage left us as the bell rang outside. All of a sudden, the joyful buzz of children playing and chattering receded as they hurried to their first Roll-Call classes. It was a small secondary school with only eight classes from first to fourth year. Most of those had far less than the usual thirty-odd students. That was a good thing from a teaching viewpoint. The trouble was, at this present rate of decline, the school wouldn't be viable in another few years and that would be terrible for the local community.

'You wanted a word, Mr Lawson?' I prompted our head, leaning back against the wooden chair at my desk.

Kenneth Lawson smiled but he appeared more like a beady-eyed Tassie Devil eying up his next meal. He slicked back an awkward strand of Brylcreem-coated hair from his bare forehead.

'I wonder, how are you finding life in our fair school so far, Miss Winters?'

I was wary. He was slinking slowly towards me.

8

'OK, I guess. Early days. The kids seem great, but obviously I don't know them yet. I still haven't met my First Form class.'

'Ah yes. 1A. I taught some of them when I was deputy at All Saints Primary across the road. Challenging is the word, but you'll see soon enough. What I really wished to discuss was your . . . em . . . appearance.'

I crossed my arms across my chest. 'Oh?'

'I am aware that it's 1973 but this isn't Sydney or even Hobart. I don't approve of my staff bleaching their hair and, considering that we have hormonal young adolescent boys here, I . . . well, quite frankly, your skirts are far too short. School uniform regulations state no higher than two inches above the knee and yours are, I'm guessing, at least six.' Suddenly he produced a roll-up tape measure and moved closer.

I let him have it! If this was what I had to put up with, then All Saints could keep their poxy job!

'Mr Lawson. If you dare try to

9

measure the length of my skirt, you'll be speaking in a squeaky voice for the next week! If you want to complain about me tempting the boys by dressing provocatively, I suggest you should have had a word with Miss Vickers and her penchant for décolletage or, as you one-track-minded men would say, 'cleavage'.' I chose not to mention that Miss Vickers was almost retirement age. 'As for dyeing my hair, I'm a natural blonde. You should direct your attentions to Mr Morris. I believe he has more Kiwi polish on his hair than on his shoes!'

I'd raised my voice considerably, unperturbed by speaking to the head this way. If I were a student, I'd have been expelled, but right now, I didn't care.

'I'm a bloody good teacher and while I'm here, I intend to educate my pupils to the best of my ability. However, I will not be patronised, especially by you. The boyfriend I left to come here tried to take me for granted, having an affair with a married woman. I won't put up with garbage from him, and I'm damned sure I won't take it from you!' I paused for breath. 'Do I resign right now or do you want to sack me? Or shall I get on and do what you employed me to do? Your choice.'

There was a moment of electrified silence.

I'd pushed him, probably far too far. I could see the shock in his eyes.

Then he moved back to sit in one of my colleagues' chairs. When he did speak there was a change in his expression that I'd never expected in a million years.

'I apologise most sincerely, Miss Winters. I've upset you by behaving appallingly. I must confess, I have never been spoken to in that way in my entire professional life. It was . . . wonderfully refreshing.' He gave me a warm grin.

I turned my head slightly to one side, quizzically.

'I'm sorry. Did . . . did you just test me out?'

He snickered to himself. 'Yes. And you passed with flying colours. Welcome to All Saints, Miss Winters. May I call you Debra?'

I nodded. 'I don't suppose you'd care to enlighten me what that charade was all about?'

'Perhaps in the next few days. Suffice it to say, I look forward to you being a valued part of All Saints for some time to come. As for the tape measure . . . ' He put it back in his pocket. 'I don't think we'll be needing that again.'

2

My life was already complicated enough without more intrigue. Granted, it seemed like this was a twist for the good but starting at a new school was always stressful, whether you were a student or a teacher.

My first task as new head of English was to assess the writing capabilities of my charges. As there was only one full-time English teacher — me — the title sounded more grandiose than it was.

Teaching this subject was a balancing act. There were so many rules and aspects to appreciation of fine literature, I sometimes felt a massive responsibility to get it right for every student. Imagination was something to be applauded, but without spelling and a working knowledge of grammar, my students might forever flounder to express themselves later in life.

'See those cockatoos on that ghost gum outside.' Twenty-two heads turned to the window. 'I want you to be like them when they fly, each with their own adventure but working together to find food and stay safe. Stretch your wings but remember you're a part of a flock . . . this class.'

One of the girls put her hand up. She was already taller than all the boys but didn't seem self-conscious about it. That was good.

'Miss Jenkins. Your question?' I said.

'Not a question, just a comment, Miss. I think one of those cockatoos has sneaked into our class room.' She indicated a boy whose hair was sticking up on top. He'd been trying to smooth it down through the lesson but had failed miserably.

The class had a good-natured laugh then the boy joined in with a cockatoo-like squawk.

As they settled down, I asked him his name.

'Kelly, Miss.'

'That's your surname. What's your first name?'

'Thomas . . . er, Tom. Why, Miss?'

I took a deep breath. What I was going to do would upset the establishment, big-time. I'd been teaching for three years and every teacher I'd known insisted on addressing pupils by their surnames. It was 'Come here, Wilkins!' or 'Straighten your tie, Smith.' Occasionally they would defer to the more polite 'Mister Wilkins' or 'Miss Smith'. I wanted to change that.

'May I call you Tom? In fact, I'd like to use all your first names in class. And before you say anything, just to let you know, my name is Debra. It goes without saying though, that you must address me as Miss Winters, or simply Miss.'

There was an immediate buzz from my flabbergasted pupils. I remembered years ago we always strived to learn our teachers' first names though we would never dare use it to their faces.

'Miss?' A girl's hand was raised.

15

'Yes, Marcia?' I'd checked my written seating plan as I'd not learned many names as yet.

She stood, nervously looking around. 'Miss Winters. I . . . I think I can speak for us all. It'd be really fab for you to use our first names but . . . but, are you sure? The other teachers . . . Mr Lawson . . . they won't approve. It's too in . . . intim . . . '

'Intimate?'

Marcia agreed, sitting down.

I smiled. 'Let me worry about that. I'm a big girl now and I can fight my own battles. It might sound like boasting, but I usually win. Are we agreed, then? My class, my rules? Marcia? Tom? Now, let's get on with the lesson.'

I noticed a change in their bored expressions immediately. Time to start.

The standard exercise that was usually given was *What would I like to be when I grow up?* My challenge was *What I don't wish to be when I grow up — and why.* I wanted to push them — more crucially, I wanted them to

16

push themselves. Quite a few sat musing intently, Biros in mouths before beginning to scribble madly.

I wandered around, sneaking peeks and gently correcting glaring mistakes while encouraging them to push their skills to the limit. If they wanted to use a big word but weren't certain how to spell it, I'd offer a dictionary. It wasn't an exercise in criticism and I sensed it was a far cry from their previous teacher's approach.

I noticed that, even though this was the top First Form class, a good half dozen were far from the base standard for eleven and twelve years old. Handwriting and simple spelling skills were poor. I realised they'd be struggling in every subject. Already their self-esteem would be suffering.

One child had written, '*I don't wanna work picking apples like my brothers,*' and was sitting back, thinking that was enough.

'That's OK, Jake, but I'd like more. Write down your reasons. As much as you can. I'd like to get to know you. Writing to me helps do that. Imagine we're just talking and write it down.'

He looked across at me kneeling by his desk.

'It's hard, Miss. I ain't very bright.'

'I understand, but there are no right or wrong answers and no marks out of ten. Just do your best. That's all I want.'

When I noticed him again, he was doing exactly that. They all were, bless them. To me, however, it was a realisation that I was going to have my teaching work cut out for me.

★ ★ ★

My free period meeting with the American, Doris, was productive. There was a Fire Safety Plan already. It needed updating to include the science lab and woodwork/metalwork rooms built ten years earlier when All Saints had been a thriving school. The procedure was simple. Any fire in any room should have the fire alarms pressed immediately. They were

18

protected by a glass cover which would be broken by the teacher in the room. An orderly evacuation to the Fire Assembly Point in the main playground would be followed by a roll-call from the attendance books. The deputy headmaster would notify the local volunteer fire brigade.

'One problem, Debra. We don't have a deputy.'

I hadn't realised it before. The headmaster was currently acting in both capacities.

'What about the senior secretary, then?' I said. 'Mrs . . . ?'

'Alliprandi.'

'We'll need to do an inventory of flammable materials too. They should be in secure metal cabinets that are kept locked.'

Doris seemed puzzled.

I tried to elaborate. 'Science labs have methylated spirits, sodium, acetone — and don't forget the concentrated acids. Then there are cleaning fluids, plus petrol for the mowers, solvents and oil-based paints in Art. Perhaps we should ask each department to do an inventory for us, along with safety precautions?'

Doris was sceptical. 'I don't fancy your chances there, kiddo. You'd be hard pressed to get any of the others to do anything but the bare minimum. Maybe Ken could ask but even so . . . '

She'd called him Ken, not Kenneth.

Suddenly, I understood. 'You knew what he was going to do, didn't you?'

'His little act, yeah. He asked me to play along. Told me he was going to put some pressure on you to see how you'd react. He was extremely pleased that you'd applied to teach here and has been pretending to be an obnoxious idiot right from your interview.'

We were the only two in the staff room. 'Tell me what's going on.'

'Ken's been struggling to improve All Saints for years but his hands have been tied with the staff. In the States, we call it tenure.'

'You mean, he's stuck with all these older teachers? Can't get rid of them?'

'Yes, not that old is bad but this lot are set in their ways. Nothing changes in their lessons. Half the kids have mentally died of boredom before they get to Third Form.'

It was as I'd suspected.

Doris continued. 'Inertia. They've been here for so long, they can't be bothered. I tried to stir things up but, like Ken, I found it a soul-destroying battle. The only way things will change is when the old fogies decide to retire — though, by then, All Saints will be closed.' She reached over to grasp my hands in hers. 'You, Debra. You're a breath of fresh air in a very stale and decaying school. I heard what you're doing with the First Formers — first names in class — golly gee! You planning the same with your other classes?'

'Yep. All of them.'

Doris patted her bright copper hair, neatly tied in a bun. Her blue eyes sparkled. 'I might give it a go too. Always seemed old-fashioned to use just surnames, but that's Tasmania, I guess.

Where I come from in Nebraska, it was much different to here. And coming Down Under . . . well, that was a shock to the system, for sure. You Aussies might be familiar with how us Yanks speak from watching movies and shows like *Bonanza*, but when I came here, it was like some foreign lingo! And you drive on the wrong side of the road!'

I laughed, then checked my watch. The staffroom clock wasn't right — for some bizarre reason! I guess I'd fix it later before Ken did. It was time for lunch, then playground duty for the second half of our fifty-minute lunchtime — salmon sarnie and a Pepsi, organised by the volunteer mums in the school canteen.

'I tell you one thing, Doris. I'm going to have to find some digs around here. That drive to Hobart and back takes me an hour each way. Any suggestions?'

'The hotel? Or what you call a pub over here. I stayed there for a few weeks before I found my one-bed place to rent.'

Inwardly I shuddered. Although I drank

socially, usually a shandy, there was no possibility of me staying there. Call me a stuck-up woman if you like, but in my experience those hotel rooms should be condemned. My last experience gave me fleas for a fortnight afterwards!

Doris saw me wince. 'Yeah, dire. Those shared bathrooms — not a pleasant experience!'

I decided to change the topic. 'Do you miss Nebraska, Doris?'

'It comes and goes. What I wouldn't give for a runza though. It's a type of sandwich — beef, cabbage, onions. I tried making my own but it wasn't the same.' She seemed a little upset, dabbing her eye. 'I have a question for you though, Debra. I heard the kids calling me Meggsie. I guess it's my nickname. Is it insulting?'

I broke out into a wide grin. 'Not at all. It's a comment on your red hair, that's all. There's a comic character who's a . . . well, he gets into trouble a bit. He's a boy with ginger hair and he's called Ginger Meggs.'

Doris smiled. 'I can live with that. I was afraid to ask anyone else. I've not made any real friends since I arrived last year.'

I felt sorry for her. Tasmania had a shortage of trained teachers and had recruited from America. It hadn't been a great success, but a few, like Doris, had decided to stay and make our island state their home.

I checked my new battery watch again, then grabbed my hat as the end of period five bell sounded. It'll be good to get outside even though it was stinking hot — twenty-eight in the shade. Even so, it would be a darn sight better than the foul odour of cigarettes and cigars that some of the teachers chose to smoke in the staff room.

'I like your hat, Debra. Very Aussie. All you need are some corks hanging off the rim.'

I posed in front of the mirror with my Akubra hat, before donning my sunnies. Maybe not haute couture, but it'd keep the burning Tassie sun off my face.

The ozone layer was thinner over Tasmania than most other places in Oz, meaning twenty-eight here was as fierce as thirty-eight in Sydney. And that protective layer of air was getting thinner. 'See you later, Doris.'

'Yeah. Or as you Aussies say, 'Ooroo'!' She gave me a cheeky grin.

I'd be teaching the last three periods of the day, but that firefighter bloke was coming for the last half of period eight. That would be good. Perhaps I'd learn something. After all I was in the countryside now, far from the bushfire-free cities of Hobart and Launceston where I'd lived all my life. It must be a concern for people out here, especially with the Fire Danger signs all indicating red Extreme. As far as our guest went, hopefully he wouldn't be an elderly cigar-smoking local!

★ ★ ★

The afternoon lessons went smoothly and I was beginning to associate faces

25

with names. When it came to half past two, there was a knock on the door and the headmaster entered.

My students stood, as I'd asked them to do whenever we had a visitor. I think Ken was impressed. It was something I insisted on with all my classes as a courtesy. There had been a grumble or two when I'd explained my rules might differ from usual school protocol, but they were good pupils. All they needed was a guiding hand.

'Mr Lawson,' I said.

'Hello Miss Winters . . . 3B. May I introduce Mr Sanderson, our local Fire Chief?'

Whatever image I'd had in my mind vanished immediately. Rather than a balding, overweight elderly bloke, I was facing a young thirty-ish guy who obviously worked out. Piercing green eyes looked out from a tanned face — no moustache or beard that seemed to be the fashion after the Beatles' *Sergeant Pepper* album came out — just longish blond hair that looked

26

like a kookaburra's nest, it was so untidy. He had a khaki shirt on with *Fire Chief* emblazoned on the chest pocket, and epaulettes on the shoulders.

'G'day, class,' he said nervously, ignoring me. I assumed he was focused on the job in hand and, despite giving the same lecture to every other class, facing a bunch of attentive kids made the most seasoned adult a little terrified. Unless you were a teacher, of course. After Mr Lawson left, the boys and girls resumed their seats.

'I see a few familiar faces so you can all call me Robbie. Mr Sanderson's not my style. I want to tell you about what to do if there's a bushfire and then you can tell your parents. They might reckon they know everything, but trust me, they don't. You remember what happened to Bazza Griffiths last year? Own the cafe across the road?'

'Yeah,' one girl commented. 'He was a friend of my mum's.'

'He was caught out in a fire. Left it

27

too late to leave the place he was camping. The fire wasn't just coming from behind him. It was all around like a circle closing in. Even that Monaro he loved wasn't fast enough to escape.'

I gathered that quite a few of the children were aware of this from the sadness on their faces.

'Tell me, guys, what precautions do you reckon you and your families should be taking at the moment, considering the forecast is for it to get hotter with no rain in sight?' He looked around for some chalk, noticing me at last. His eyes lingered as though noticing me for the first time.

'Mrs Walker, is it?'

'Miss Winters, actually.'

'Apologies. Could you write the suggestions on the blackboard, please?'

I nodded.

Karen, with the glasses, raised her hand. 'Listen to weather warnings on the radio?'

'An excellent suggestion. You're Jack Cooper's youngest kid, aren't you? Top bloke. I remember doing some work — '

'Robbie? The list?'

'Oh yes. Sorry, Miss Winters, kids. I always got into trouble when I was your age, sat in this room, chirping away like a budgie. Some things never change! Next suggestion . . . Bluey?'

It amazed me that a red-haired guy was called Bluey. The boy, whose name I hadn't yet learned, wasn't upset.

'Have a survival kit handy, Robbie. Like um . . . a torch, battery radio, drinking water, money in case you lose your home.'

'That's dead brill, Blue. Survival kit, Miss Winters — write it down.' Then in an aside to the kids, he whispered loudly, 'Always wanted to give my teachers orders.' The class laughed. He was relaxed now he had them in the palm of his hand.

And so it went. After the list, there were questions . . . 'Have you been in many fires, Mister Robbie? Did you ever get burned?'

'Let's see . . . I don't keep count, but

more than fifty bushfires in the last fourteen years. This year looks like a bad'un. As for being hurt, no, but my big sister got burned once. That's why I joined up — to stop it happening to anyone else.'

'What's been the worst fire you've seen?' Bluey asked, pushing his glasses to the bridge of his freckled nose.

Robbie thought a bit. 'Four summers ago. Chrissie Day. Wiped out four homes at Wattle Grove. I thought it was going to get worse though, thought the winds'd pick up and we'd have a fire no one could control. We call that a firestorm — bits of burning leaves and ash blowing in all directions, igniting trees and houses for miles around. No way could we put one of them out. Lucky for us, the winds dropped and my team got it under control before we lost more homes.'

It was a sobering thought.

Just then the final bell sounded — three o'clock, and time for my pupils to go home.

I walked out to the bus queues with Robbie Sanderson. We were both wearing our leather Akubras as three o'clock seemed to be the hottest part of the day.

I decided a bit of a friendly chat was in order. 'You're only a volunteer fireman then. What's your proper job, Robbie?'

'Builder. I just became a qualified electrician too. Not a lot of work for me hereabouts so I'm branching out.'

I helped line the pupils up to catch their buses in an orderly way. They didn't need much supervision though, as they were well behaved. Besides it was too hot for them to mess around.

Robbie hung back watching until the last bus departed. Once the other staff wandered off, I returned to the Fire Chief. He seemed interesting and being out here with him was preferable to returning to the staff-room with its clouds of cigarette smoke. He was standing in the shade of a ghost gum, leaning indifferently against the trunk, long khaki socks and shorts matching his shirt. A typical rugged Aussie male.

I wandered over to him. 'Is being a fireman exciting?' I asked, immediately regretting my stupid question.

'Wouldn't say exciting. Terrifying at times. Gets the adrenalin pumping for sure. Fire . . . she's very primeval. We've learned to harness her for keeping warm in winter and cooking food but she's always ready to break out from man-made prisons and wreak havoc. We can never tame her, despite all our civilisation.'

'You call fire 'she'. Any reason for that?'

Robbie mopped the sweat from his brow with a hanky, musing on the answer.

'Dunno. Maybe a shrink would say there's some kind of man-woman relationship between me and her, fighting all the time. I've had a few volatile girlfriends in the past, ready to hit the bloody roof if I didn't treat them just the way they wanted. On the other hand, my big sis, Wendy's into stars and astrology and stuff. She reckons fire signs are female. Do you believe in that stuff, Miss Winters?'

'Debra, please. If you're asking me to accept that the horoscopes in the paper predict that all Scorpios will be lucky in love tomorrow, no, I don't. Newspaper astrology is for the gullible, people who think thirteen is unlucky. Saying that, I do know there's more to astrology than Sun signs.'

'Do you know the different signs of the Zodiac?' Robbie asked.

'Aries, Leo the Lion, Sagittarius the Archer . . . I'm an Aries, a Ram . . . one of those people who supposedly charge into things, act before I think. Aries is a fire sign.'

'Just my luck, then,' Robbie chuckled. 'Meeting the personification of the thing I must fight. Doesn't matter though. This conversation is a one-off. You're new here in The Valley. Once you hear the gossip about me — and you will — you'll probably never speak to me again. Certainly not friendly like this.'

I was shocked but tried not to show it. Not that I was searching for a relationship now but Robbie seemed to be on the same wavelength, someone I could at least be friends with.

'Do I seem that judgemental?' I asked him, trying to break the sudden tension.

'Crikey, no. But people will tell you all sorts about me, most of it true when I was younger. No self-respecting woman would bother. Pleased to meet you, though. Hope it works out for you here.' With those strange final words, he turned and left me wondering what had just happened.

3

Trying not to dwell on Robbie's words, I made my way back to the staff room. The yard was strangely quiet with the students gone. Our caretaker waved as he collected the bins of rubbish strategically placed around the concrete playground. The grassed area for footie and cricket games was now a dust bowl with only brown clumps of leaves to show where the grass had once been. A willy-willy swirled around and headed my way, blowing choking dust into my mouth and eyes. It was just like a ghost town from the Westerns I'd watched as a girl.

'There you are,' Doris cried out from the covered veranda outside the science laboratory. 'Thought you forgotten.'

I dusted myself off. The dirt was worse than chalk dust for clinging to clothes. 'Sorry. Was having a chin-wag with the Fire Chief. Strange guy. Do you know anything about him?'

'No. Afraid not. I'll ask my landlady. She's almost a local, been here forty years. Shall we check this Fire Precaution stuff out? I've looked at the science lab, and the gas bottles are in a locked cage outside the building.'

That made sense. They'd use the gas for the Bunsen burners. 'I read the old guidelines. Every classroom should have a fire blanket easily accessible as well as two fire extinguishers, one powder for electrical and a carbon dioxide one. We need to record when they were last checked. Thanks for helping me with this, Doris.'

'Think of it as gossip time. There's lots you need to know about life out here in the bush if you're gonna survive. Perhaps we can be friends.'

'Sounds good to me, Meggsie.'

★ ★ ★

An hour later I was on my way back to Hobart. Thank goodness I'd bought an

36

air-conditioned car, but even so, the vinyl seat burned the back of my legs when I got in. I'd have to remember to park on the other side of the car park, under the shade of the jacarandas.

It'd be a long drive back so I put a cassette in the player connected to the radio. The music I grew up with was my favourite, though I still kept up to date with modern groups. The cassette was one I'd made up from the vinyl 45s I'd collected avidly in the 60s. Immediately the thumping sounds of *Bits and Pieces* by the Dave Clark Five filled my car, relaxing me in spite of the thumping beat. I guess it took me back to happier times when I still believed in the happy ever after of falling in love.

I switched on the ignition after pulling out the choke. Lulu spluttered, once . . . twice . . . then died. Someone had suggested the battery needed changing. The stuff under the bonnet was a mystery to me. With all that'd happened these past few weeks, getting a new battery had been the last of my concerns. I switched off the music and turned the ignition.

'Come on, Lulu, be a good girl for Mummy.'

Talking to my car wasn't logical but if it worked, I didn't care. It spluttered again, making a whirring noise I realised wasn't good. Then, just as I was about to release the starter, it caught.

'Thank you, little car,' I told her, nursing the choke. 'This weekend, Mummy will get you fixed up, Lulu. Promise.'

Doing this hundred-odd mile trip every day wouldn't do her any good at all — or me for that matter.

It was totally down to me breaking up with Shane. I'd just given notice on my rented unit prior to moving in with Shane — the same time I discovered what he'd been up to and had broken up with him. Unfortunately, it left me without a home and, given that Shane was my boss at school, I had no choice but to leave my teaching position too. My life had been in turmoil. No place to stay and I had to find a job. The digs

38

with my Uni friend near the market in Hobart was temporary.

Now, I turned into Koala Avenue then Bandicoot Way. Whoever had named the streets in this town had a strange fascination with Aussie animals.

Although Australia had gone metric last year, most of us still thought in miles or pounds. Leaving the town boundaries, the speed limit signs had been changed just last week to kilometres per hour. Progress? I guessed it was.

It wasn't long before I was on the way back to Huonville, the biggest town in the Huon Valley. There the road from Hobart split, one side crossing the Huon River and heading south with the river on the left. The other road headed left and took you down the eastern side of the river. Even being the hub of The Valley, the population was less than two thousand.

When *Any Way You Want It* came over the speakers, I sang along. Shane choosing to have an affair with the headmaster's wife had been upsetting to say the least but I'd get over it. I'd always been a glass half-full type of woman, searching for the best in any situation. After all, even if I'd thought Shane was my soulmate, at least we weren't hitched. We didn't have to split the proceeds from selling a house. As for the money he'd cleared out of our joint account, I was sure he'd return it . . . fingers crossed. In fact, him stealing that money probably hurt more than betraying me with an older woman.

All around the car, people were waving and pointing at me. With a shock, I realised I was on Huonville's main street, still singing along, obviously loudly enough to be heard. I waved back, trying to forget what Shane had done. I managed to keep kidding myself until I could pull over to the side of the road where only thousands of apple trees standing mutely in their rows could see me cry. No amount of feelgood music could help me now.

'Damn you, Shane! Damn you to hell!'

I switched off the music while staring out at the miles of orchards that encompassed the Huon Highway. This valley was the heart of Australia's apple industry. In the distance there was Sleeping Beauty, one of the mountains of the range between The Valley and Hobart. I dried my eyes and was about to put my sunnies back on when there was a loud tapping on my window.

I almost jumped out of my skin. A tanned face with aviator sunglasses peered back at me sternly. Blue lights were flashing in my rear vision mirror. Police. Winding down the window, I asked what the problem was.

'No problem, Miss. Just noticed you pulled up on the hard shoulder and wondered if you'd broken down,' he replied. From his chevrons I saw he was a sergeant. His distinctive blue shirt and holstered gun reminded me that Aussie police were more like their American counterparts than the unarmed British bobby.

41

'Sorry. Just having a bit of a cry. Man troubles,' I explained, a little embarrassed. 'I'll be OK. Thanks for your concern, officer.'

He gave a forced smile, said goodbye and was about to leave when he spied the books spilling out of my case onto the passenger seat. The school crest was on the cover of my student's exercise books.

'Are you that new teacher at All Saints?'

'Yes, I am, Sergeant. Debra Winters.'

'Senior Sergeant Powell, Miss Winters. I should have recognised you from my daughter's description. She said you look like a movie star.'

I grinned. 'What — Lassie?' My hair did have a certain resemblance to the hero dog's.

'More like Brigitte Bardot. Heather reckons you're 'bad', which I gather means great. Her word, not mine.' He'd removed his glasses and his friendliness was pleasingly genuine.

'That's nice to know. Heather's very

mature for her age. Not that I've taught her much.'

I checked the time. I had a lot of marking to do and it was getting on. I did feel better though — well enough to drive home.

'I really should be going, Senior Sergeant.'

He stood back. 'Sure. And my name's Chris.' He held his hand out to shake mine. I had to twist around, but I grasped his before we said farewell.

Peering back in the rear-view mirror I saw him waving from the police Monaro. It was an unusual gesture for an officer, especially a high-ranking one. Time for some more music, I thought, feeling quite perky again. When the Cicadas began singing *That's What I Want*, I chose to add my terrible singing voice to theirs.

★ ★ ★

It was an easy drive traffic-wise. Weaving around the winding roads below

Mount Wellington was the worst part, then it was a downhill drive into Hobart. Carrie-Anne's townhouse backed onto Salamanca market. It was small — I think the polite word was 'bijou' — with an open plan kitchen/lounge/diner on the first floor and two bedrooms and a bathroom on the top. A double garage and toilet were downstairs.

I settled down at the dining table and began reading the essays from three of my classes. I had no intention of correcting every spelling or grammatical error, though I'd obviously discuss common ones for the respective classes. As expected, these students had different attitudes and life experiences to the Hobart school where I'd previously taught. That wasn't a problem.

I put the papers down after finishing, then grabbed a Pepsi from the fridge. I rarely drank hot drinks of any kind apart from hot chocolate. Mum said my taste buds had never matured like normal people's. The same applied to wine — it tasted vile and I never understood the attraction. I reckoned it was like opera. People thought it made them more sophisticated, and they pretended to like it, like the Emperor's New Clothes.

Carrie-Anne came upstairs from the garage at about quarter to seven with two bags of groceries. Rushing over to help her, we put the groceries away then I paid her for my half.

'I see you've been busy making a mess again.' She nodded at the stacks of exercise books. 'What are they like? Any budding Shakespeareans?' Carrie-Anne worked in the Commonwealth Bank on Elizabeth Street.

'Not too bad, except for five of the First Formers. Their English is well behind and it's not because they have low IQs. It's a puzzle.'

'One I'm sure you'll solve. You always were great at explaining things. Oh, before I forget, I saw Shane at the shops. Says he misses you.'

'Yeah, right,' I retorted dismissively. 'He wants you to go back to his place. He's finished up with that woman.'

That was a surprise.

'For what it's worth, Debbie, I don't think you should. The bloke's sneakier than a Tassie Devil crawling under the wire of a chook pen.'

There was no possibility I'd return to Shane, not after what he'd done. For the same reason, I couldn't return to the school where he'd been my boss. Even though moving schools had been a last-minute panic, I had a feeling it'd be for the best, but I had to find accommodation closer to All Saints. In two weeks Carrie-Anne's brother would be back to restart Uni and he wouldn't take kindly to sharing his tiny room with me!

We decided to head down to Constitution Docks for fish and chips, where Carrie-Anne noticed smoke from the side of Mount Wellington. The red glow was still there at night when I woke and peered outside, though the brush fire had gone by morning. The

46

firemen had done their job of controlling this outbreak.

As I drove to school on Friday morning, I saw the blackened forest in the distance. So much devastation. Then I remembered something Robbie had said to the class . . .

'Kids, there's no rain in sight and the weather guys are predicting a heatwave this month. Sadly, all these bushfires around Tassie are going to get much worse.'

'Worse than the fires of '67?' one of the girls had asked. We all remembered them. Sixty-four people died, over nine hundred were injured and our heavily forested state lost tens of thousands of acres to the flames of Black Tuesday.

'Let's pray not,' Robbie had concluded soberly.

At that moment I'd realised he must have been one of those brave firefighters trying to protect us while my younger self had watched the events of that horrendous day unfold on the telly.

By the beginning of the third period, it was clear today would be another stinking hot day. The temperature gauge in our classroom was already reading 31C/ 88F. My windows were open in the hope there'd be some cooling breeze, but there wasn't. All the fans overhead could do was circulate the already stifling air around us.

I was teaching my First Form class some fun poetry called Haiku and asked them to compose their own versions. They all seemed to be rising to the challenge so I took a moment to drink some water from a bottle in my bag.

One girl put up her hand. 'Could I have some water too, Miss. It's very hot.'

'Of course, you can. You don't need to ask.' Looking around at their flagging faces, I saw perspiration on many brows and they looked surprised. Clearly it wasn't normally acceptable to drink during lessons. That was barbaric.

I clapped my hands for attention.

'Listen up, class. You all have permission to drink from your water bottles in class. Water, fruit juice or cordial. I do not want any of you being dehydrated or melting away. No soft drinks bottles or cans — and definitely no beer.'

There was a buzz of laughter and my twelve-year old pupils all took their plastic water bottles out to drink. A few had clearly been very thirsty!

Maxine raised her hand. I nodded to her to give her permission to speak.

'But Miss. None of the other teachers . . .'

I tapped the blackboard where I had written my motto in coloured chalk: *My classroom, my rules.* The boys and girls nodded in understanding. Not that I was a soft teacher. If anyone didn't conform to my high expectations of courtesy, I would gently remind them who was boss.

As they began to resume their

exercise, I had one more thing to say.

'Class, as I've told you all before, I don't wish to hear you complaining that other staff should do the same as me. Their classrooms, their rules. Remember that. But when you're here with me . . . ' I tapped the board again.

After a while, I asked them to put their pens down. It was time to hear what gems they'd managed to write. One by one they stood and read, the class giving each a polite clap at the end and offering positive feedback. It was all about encouragement.

Unfortunately, when it came to Tom's turn, he was clearly reluctant. In spite of my entreaties, he gave up after a few words of faltering pronunciation. It was then I understood his self-esteem was low because of his struggles expressing himself.

When class was dismissed for recess, I stopped him for a moment, waiting until the others were gone. 'Tom. I'm sorry I made you feel uncomfortable earlier.'

He shifted on his feet, uneasily. 'Not

your fault, Miss. Told you I was a drongo.'

I had a proposition. 'I can help you with your reading. We can start this lunchtime if you don't mind spending it with me. You see, Tom. I loved your essay about not wanting to be like your dad and I'd love you to read it to the class after lunch.'

He stared at me, horrified.

'You can do it. Just join me here for lunch, please. At least it will be cooler in here than in the playground and, if I can't help you, you don't need to read at all. Is that OK?'

It took a few seconds before he agreed. My plan might backfire but it was worth a try.

★   ★   ★

The staff room was buzzing with voices when I entered. Some student had seemingly turned up today for the first time this year. He was universally disliked. Archie pointed him out to me in the playground. He wasn't wearing a

51

uniform and was pushing a couple of smaller boys.

'Freddie Belfour. He's a right little thug. We had a ding-dong in Art this morning. Ended up caning him — for all the good it will do.'

I didn't approve of corporal punishment, but that was me.

Doris joined as we watched him, yelling at some girls across the courtyard. I assumed it was foul language from the expressions on their faces.

'Not as little now. He'll be worse now he's an adolescent. You should be grateful he's not in any of your classes, Debra. Disruptive and rude, especially to women.'

Normally I don't prejudge anyone, but in this case, I took note of the unanimously negative comments about young Freddie.

* * *

When lunchtime came, I stayed in my classroom to eat. Tom was prompt,

52

knocking politely before entering. He was anxious but keen to at least try.

'Firstly, I'd like you to read your excellent composition to me. There's only the two of us.'

I gave him his exercise book and his face lit up. 'How come it's not covered with red pen, Miss?'

'Because I think we should concentrate on improving your English bit by bit. Read what you've written about your father and why you don't want to be like him.'

The essay wasn't angry or hateful. It simply described a man who had accepted his life without trying to change it. Tom wanted to travel to the mainland and other countries. His dad had apparently never gone further than Hobart. The composition showed that Tom loved his parents, and they him, but he had ambition to make something of himself. He wanted to be a pilot.

His parents had been raised in a more restrictive environment. All that generation had.

Tom read slowly and hesitantly, stumbling over multi-syllabled words. Sentence by sentence I read them prior to asking Tom to repeat his words until his confidence grew. I acknowledged to myself it would be cheating a little when he read his composition to the class — he'd almost memorised it — but now he had a much better concept of intonation, how to raise and lower his voice and pause at commas.

We could work on the basic stuff in other lunchtimes when I wasn't on playground duty. I didn't mind helping him — it was my job. For some reason he and some others had fallen behind in second or third class back at Primary and they'd never caught up. He had the potential to do so — all he needed was a patient, guiding hand.

★ ★ ★

Period six began, and it was hotter than ever.

Pony-tailed Janet started off reading

her composition about how she didn't want to be a housewife washing clothes and yukky nappies. 'Women should be able to do the same jobs as men,' she concluded, receiving applause for her articulate piece of work.

I noticed one boy sniggering to his mate.

'Nigel, isn't it? Something you'd care to share with the rest of the class?'

He stood up. 'Not being rude, Miss, but sheilas can't do muscular work like blokes.' Glancing around for moral support, only one boy nodded.

I took my time answering. 'Nigel. I believe that Janet wasn't suggesting that all women can physically do all that men can. There are differences that I'm sure you are aware of. However, Janet believes — and I agree with her — that women should be given the opportunity, the choice, to do whatever job they want. The world is changing. For instance, when I was your age, I wanted to be a firewoman or a policewoman. Instead I ended up here. It was my choice. I have a girlfriend who's training to be a helicopter pilot and another is captain of a yacht that competed in the Sydney-Hobart yacht race last year.'

'I didn't mean . . . ' Nigel began, apologetically.

'I realise that, Nigel. You're entitled to your opinion, which I respect even if I don't agree with it. But there is one thing I do take exception to.'

My eyes fixed him with my best stern and disapproving stare.

He swallowed. 'What's that, Miss?'

My voice was measured yet firm. 'I never, ever wish to hear that disgusting term 'sheila' used by you or anyone in this class again. Is that clear?'

His reply was meek. 'Yes, Miss.'

'Very good, Nigel. Please sit down. We'll say no more about it. Next essay please? Any volunteers? How about you, Nigel? I really enjoyed your composition about wanting to work on a farm.' He seemed surprised but accepted my invitation, any hard feelings soon forgotten.

At last it came to Tom's turn to read. He did an impressive job, accepting the extended claps by his classmates. His beaming face showed me more than words ever could.

As he took his seat, I noticed movement outside over near the Art Block. All the students and teachers should have been in class and the toilets were at the other end of the school. There was no Art lesson at the moment.

A figure emerged from the Art Room, closing the door behind him. He had paint on his jeans and shirt. I recognised him as Freddie, the so-called trouble-maker. By this time, some of the students had noticed my preoccupation and were half standing, two of the girls joining me at the window.

Something wasn't right. He should have been in class. Moreover, the way he was moving was furtive with constant glances all around. When he saw us, Freddie began to sprint, disappearing behind the Home Economics block.

'Miss,' one of the girls exclaimed,

pointing. I followed her hand, not seeing anything. 'Smoke, Miss. There's a fire!'

She was right. Thin wisps of smoke were visible, beginning to thicken then billow from an open window. Immediately I ran to the other side of my room, smashing the fire alarm glass with my closed fist. Instead of blaring klaxons or bells, there was nothing. No sound at all.

'Everyone out,' I shouted. 'Fire drill. Assemble outside of Mr Lawson's office. Leave all your belongings. Go — quickly!'

It wasn't the agreed Assembly Point and I knew it. Nevertheless, it was the safest point. There were gas bottles for the Art Room kiln not three metres from the smoke that was becoming even more dense.

I spoke to the two more mature girls who had been by my side. 'Sarah. Run to Mr Lawson and tell him there's a fire in the Art Room and I'm trying to deal with it. The fire alarms aren't working.

Tell him that too.' She disappeared through the door. 'Jennifer. Go to all the teachers and tell them what's happening. Start with Miss de Shannon — and move them away from this part. Quickly, please.'

Fortunately, my classroom was at the far end of the school. This real emergency highlighted a great number of problems with the existing escape arrangements. And how the hell could the fire alarms be broken? The lives of children depended on it! Normally, I'd follow procedures and evacuate to a safe point but the proximity of those two huge gas cylinders so close to the seat of the fire concerned me. Perhaps the fire over there was small enough to contain. I grabbed the two fire extinguishers from their wall brackets and carried them to the veranda across the play area. No one was nearby but I could hear the sound of the other classes leaving their classrooms.

The Art Room door was ajar and, peeking in, I saw the glow of flames through the smoke. It appeared to be inside a storage cupboard on the far side by the blackboard. Such places generally had no windows. The acrid smoke had thinned out, drawn through the open classroom windows.

Already my eyes were stinging. It was difficult to breathe. On impulse, I grabbed a towel, wet it under a tap then tied it loosely over my nose and mouth. Only at that point did I dare enter the storeroom. The fire was in a metal bin, piled high with flaming shreds of rags.

Fire blanket! I thought, kicking myself for not bringing one. There'd be one in this classroom though. I found it rapidly then returned to the store room just as some spilt liquid on a shelf burst into flame. Damn! First things first — the bin. Throwing the blanket over the top immediately smothered the main fire but the burning liquid was spreading along the wooden shelves toward the door which was the only way out. I grabbed an extinguisher off the floor just as sparks ignited a pool of mineral turps on the floor.

'Come on — work!' I yelled, my voice muffled by the towel. The bloody thing was empty!

Grabbing the other one, I frantically tried the trigger of that. A small amount of foam hissed out before it too died.

I had no choice now. I had to get through the exit before I was cut off completely. Fire was lapping across three shelves and the lino floor was melting in parts. My heart was racing as I carefully shuffled between the stifling flames and smoke. Somewhere behind there was a tiny explosion as something ignited.

'Debra! You in there?' Doris called. 'Get out! It's too dangerous!'

'Coming!' I yelled back, choking on smoke. Another foot or two . . . then the door closed in my face with a bang! The latch had engaged and it wouldn't push open no matter how hard I tried.

'No!' I screamed, reaching for the door handle. I couldn't see it so I fumbled up and down the heavy door. Then the blackness parted for a moment as I stared at the blistering yellow paint on the door's inside. I was doomed to die here, trapped, because I couldn't open the damn door — there was no doorknob!

4

The smoke had nowhere to go now and my makeshift mask was drying out quickly, allowing the noxious stuff to get into my mouth and nose. I realised the oxygen was being gobbled up by the fire itself. I tried to scream but it was impossible. All around was the sound of crackling flames coming ever closer.

Someone was banging on the door, yelling. I bashed my closed fists back at them, feeling the door begin to open. Bracing myself, I pushed it hard, and it caved in! I rushed out of the room, desperately gasping for fresh air.

Doris led me outside where I put my hands on my knees, coughing. 'The fire!' I gasped.

'Ken has extinguishers. The brigade's on their way. Heavens above, what were you thinking?'

'The . . . the door was open when I

63

went in. My extinguishers . . . they were empty.'

'Let's check you over.' She moved around me. 'Looks OK, but there are singe marks all over your clothes. You were lucky.'

I stood up as Ken emerged from the still smouldering building. He flung the fire extinguisher to one side. 'Only half full but I think the flames are out now.'

Two firemen ran up from the appliance. Ken pointed and they went inside, dragging a hose.

It was only then that my boss turned to me.

Doris appraised him of my condition. 'She's been lucky, Ken. Still need to have her checked out at the local clinic though. Smoke inhalation?'

He made his own cursory assessment, showing more concern that I would have expected from someone who'd only known me a few days. Clearly, I'd misjudged him. 'What you did was nothing short of extremely brave, Debra. Either that or foolhardy.

I'm still deciding which.'

Only then did I have a chance to consider what had happened. Most of the fire had been suppressed by the blanket, and I could have dealt with the rest if the door hadn't blown shut.

'It was . . . that Freddie boy. I saw . . . saw him running away.'

'One of the girls said so. Police are on their way, Debra, rest assured. We're grateful you acted so quickly. If those gas bottles had become too hot . . .' We all paused, understanding the potential catastrophe.

We needed to talk about the useless alarm and firefighting equipment but that could wait. There was a more pressing matter I needed to share with Ken, and for some reason, I thought it best not to share my concerns with Doris.

'Doris, could you tell everyone it's safe to return to classes?' Not that much teaching would get done in the seventy-odd minutes until home time but it would be too difficult to arrange buses to come earlier than their allocated time. Playing sporting games was out of the question in this oppressive heat.

She turned to Ken, who agreed. 'Do as Debra asked, please. Tell whoever has a free period to take her class this afternoon. Our English mistress is in no state to teach. Ask the secretaries to be prepared for calls from anxious parents. The official story is, we had a small fire that was dealt with promptly. No pupils were in danger.'

Doris was hardly out of earshot when Ken sat me down in the shade, vanished for a few seconds and returned with some iced water.

He sat next to me as I gratefully sipped it.

'Damned close call, Debra. But you did well.'

I leaned back against the wall. Benches in schools were uncomfortable, especially when every part of my body ached from exertion.

'Sorry about telling Doris what to do instead of waiting for you,' I apologised.

'Don't be. You saw what needed to be done and you did it. Just like raising the alarm and tackling the fire. You're a woman who takes charge when you need to.'

I turned to face him. His eyes were closed from too much Aussie sunshine and his normally neatly slicked-back hair was in disarray.

'Ken, it's not only that. I wanted to talk to you alone. I had that fire under control, and if only that door hadn't closed — ' I coughed a few times. My throat was still dry in spite of the water.

'Can't understand why you didn't prop it open.'

I paused, wiping a tear from my eye with the back of my soot-covered hand. Somehow appearances weren't that important right now, considering what I was about to say to him.

'That's exactly the thing, Ken. I realised the risk of being locked in and shoved some books in front of the door. The only way that damned door closed is if it was shut deliberately.'

★　★　★

The rest of the afternoon was a chaotic blur.

I was checked out by the doctor across the road in the clinic, no waiting around at all, I was ushered straight in.

One thing, he pointed out was my nylon blouse. It wouldn't catch alight, he said, it would melt, making any skin damage that much harder to deal with. Happily, that hadn't happened!

His main concern was my lungs. I explained about my home-made mask, and because my cough had almost gone by then, he did some breathing tests before advising that I was OK.

After that was an interview with the local Senior Constable who was quite aware of young Freddie already. He was apparently one of the area's villains-in-training. As this was arson — and possibly attempted murder — he suggested to both me and Ken that we shouldn't expect to see him back at All Saints — ever.

Ken spoke up. 'That's sad. I'd hoped to bring him around. But you're right, officer. I'm afraid he's gone too far this time.'

The police officer confided that Freddie had been suspected of other pyromania but there'd been no witnesses before. Nor had the fires been stopped in time to retrieve evidence. This time had been different.

'We found the little toe-rag's prints on the accelerant bottles he'd used. He won't be talking himself out of this one.'

I stayed late after school to assist Ken and Archie in the clean-up of the art area. The damage had been confined to the store room with some smoke and soot damage to the walls and furniture in the classroom. It would mean a major clean over the weekend, but art lessons could resume on Monday.

I went with Ken to his office after that. It was time for some serious decisions to be made in the light of the fiasco of the school's fire preparedness

— or lack thereof.

I'd be very late getting back to my temporary digs in Salamanca yet it didn't go dark until around nine. Tasmania had been the first state to introduce daylight savings in '68 and although a few people had a whinge about it, I reckoned the later sunset was well worth it.

'Why do you want me here, Ken?' I asked.

'Because I trust you, Debra. You've got more brains and common sense in your pinkie than most of the other staff have in their whole body. Or haven't you worked that out yet?'

'That's a bit harsh on them. I'll take it as a compliment but I can't judge people I hardly know — and Doris is OK.'

Ken was relaxing in a swivel chair behind an impressive but well-worn Tassie oak desk. He'd pulled a comfy armchair up next to the desk so we could both enjoy the slightly cooler breeze offered by the large fan on a stand. We still had the odd fly to deal with, attracted by our perspiration, but the smell of an insecticide was enough to keep most of the little nippers away.

Ken leaned back in a reflective mood. 'Yes. Meggsie's OK, but she has her own issues. She's a stranger in a strange land. So that's why it's you and me. Like Steed and Mrs Peel from *The Avengers*.'

I had to laugh. Me — a crime fighter? Yet we did have a crime to solve. What had happened to put the school in so much danger?

Ken reached into a drawer on the desk, producing two cans of Passiona and two Cherry Ripes. 'I noticed you're partial to a soft drink, Debra. The choccie might be a bit soft, though. Would you care to join me?'

I did. The chocolate on the Cherry Ripe was soft but perfectly acceptable.

There were two issues to address, Ken said. The non-functioning alarms and the useless empty extinguishers. I suggested a third which Ken hadn't realised. Why was the art store room door unlocked? The door hadn't been forced.

Ken made a note of that. 'Alarms . . . I did try two others, even the one in here. Nothing. I should contact the local guy who fitted it. They were signed off by an officer from the local council.'

That stunned me. 'Things like that aren't meant to go wrong, Ken. Were you there when it was tested?'

'Of course. I'll give Sparkle Sam a bell over the weekend. He put it in, so he'll fix it.'

'Personally, I don't think that's a good idea. He'll probably make up some excuse as to why there was a failure. From what I've seen I wouldn't trust him to change a light bulb.'

'Fair point. Trouble is, he's the only sparkie around here.'

I had an answer for that. 'Robbie Sanderson is a qualified electrician — or so he says — and he knows fire regs. Get him to have a look at the system. He might have some advice on the extinguishers too.'

He raised his soft drink can to me. 'Already you're there making sensible suggestions, Debra. You'll be perfect for the job I have in mind.'

'Er . . . thanks, Ken,' I replied warily. What job?

★   ★   ★

Saturday morning was spent checking out the classifieds in the Mercury. There wasn't anything suitable to rent down in The Valley — either too big (what would I do with a four-bedroom house on ten acres?) or too expensive. That thieving Shane had taken the few thousand we'd saved up in our joint account so my personal piggy bank was almost empty. I could manage a rental deposit and the first month's rent but that was about it.

As far as getting my hard-earned money back from Shane went, I'd not had a chance to make legal enquiries. It seemed as though he must have forged my signature, because the account required both to sign for any withdrawals. The bank would surely be responsible. Perhaps my present flatmate could offer advice.

Carrie-Anne had been mesmerised when I related the drama of yesterday's fire. She had been very concerned, which was comforting and showed what a great mate she was. One thing was for certain. My maroon ensemble from yesterday had seen better days. It was time for a visit to my favourite clothes stall on the market. I only had a hundred metres to walk to the bustling iconic shopping area, an advantage to staying with Carrie-Anne.

The weather was cooler with pewter grey clouds shrouding the skies. No sign of rain though, which was a concern for all us Tasmanians. Even though the bushfire threat had diminished, it was still there, ready to flare up if the fierce temperatures and winds came back.

I took my time browsing the many

craft and food stalls on the way to 'Carnaby Street'. There had been a particularly fetching linen skirt I'd noticed last time, mauve with white pleats. Fingers crossed, Colette still had it in my size. It was a midi-skirt too. Wearing a mini-skirt — a real mini-skirt — to school would have given too many of the staid staff apoplexy!

I'd just finished an ice cream as I strolled between garishly adorned stalls when I felt a tap on my shoulder. 'Fancy meeting you here,' I heard a familiar voice say. Twisting my head around, I was staring face to face with Shane. I took my glasses off. My day had suddenly been ruined, big time.

'Get lost, Shane. I don't want to speak to you.' I resumed my browsing, praying the worm would crawl off. He didn't. He persisted, shadowing me like some predator circling his prey. Suddenly I was conscious that the things I once found endearing were now downright creepy.

Time to take the offensive. 'Hello,

Shane Pendleton,' I said in my loudest voice. 'Have you come to return the money you stole from me?' A few people followed my gaze, others laughed.

Shane remained unfazed. He smiled at the onlookers. 'Lovers' tiff,' he explained confidently before whispering 'Debbs. You're embarrassing yourself. I just want a word. In private.'

He was right, we did need to talk. After the shouting match when I discovered his infidelity and told him we were finished, we hadn't spoken — a few phone calls where I'd used some unladylike words but nothing to resolve our break-up.

'OK, we can grab a drink down at the Docks. Your treat. I'm a little short of cash right now,' was my pointed concession.

'Actually, I wanted to return your money, kiddo.' It was his little-boy apologetic look. Not that I'd fall for it any more, but getting the money back without hassles was worth listening to what he had to say.

We walked briskly down the hill to Constitution Dock. The yachts from the annual Sydney-Hobart yacht race had long since set sail. Although there were people enjoying a promenade around the quay, the hustle and bustle of a month ago had gone. There were only a few people in the converted boat that now served as a restaurant on the water.

'Choccie malted milkshake for you, Debbs?'

I hated his familiarity. 'Yeah. And don't call me Debbs. You don't have that right any longer.'

He sat down with a tea and passed me my shake. 'Good to see you again,' he replied with a cheesy insincere grin. 'I love you. You know that.' I didn't respond. 'I've finished with Jane, you know. She was too demanding.'

I grinned. 'Actually, I hear she finished with you and told her hubby everything. I imagine that made it difficult for you at school, him being the headmaster and all.'

He removed his dark glasses. 'Seems like everyone knows. I'm being treated like a pariah there. But you can come back to me — and the school, they haven't replaced you yet — and I . . . well, I won't be your boss any longer. If the staff see you've forgiven me, they'll give me a second chance, I reckon.'

Revenge did a happy little dance inside my mind. 'They demoted you?'

'Yeah. That's why I need you back with me.' He donned his sunnies again. 'If you come home and back to our school, I'll give you that money back, Debb — Debra. What do you say? Are we good again? Am I forgiven?'

'Absolutely not! You hurt me, Shane, hurt me badly. I was willing to marry you then, but you're not the man I thought you were. Even now, you're only thinking about yourself, to save your reputation. As for the affair . . . the headmaster's wife, for heaven's sake? What were you thinking? I've moved on, Shane — and I *will* get my money back, count on it, Mister.'

My voice was raised more than I would have liked. We had an audience. Nevertheless, I was adamant that Shane understood we were through. I took a long slurp from the milkshake. No point in wasting it. Then I stood, grabbed my handbag from the chair and then calmly flung the rest of the milky concoction over Shane's face.

'I never want to see you again, Shane Pendleton. Never!' That brought a few gasps and claps from people seated nearby.

'Sorry,' I said to the matronly shop owner, giving her a five-dollar bill for the mess.

'Keep your money, love. I heard enough to know what he did. You're better off without him.'

'Thanks,' I said, glancing at the very soggy man I hated more than anyone. 'I just hope he gets the message this time.'

★ ★ ★

When Monday came, I made it a point to be at school early. A part of me felt responsible for the damage to the Art Room. Archie came up to me while I was peering through the window.

'Come on in, Debra. You wouldn't think it was the same place as Friday. Me and the cleaner got it spick and span. Still stinks a bit, though . . .'

The transformation was impressive. The store room was closed, but any salvageable materials were now on shelves around the classroom. Strangely, the walls were festooned with prints and student artwork.

Archie beamed. 'Reckoned the old room need a spruce up. Been a while since I bothered but, after what you did, it got me thinking.'

Outside I saw Robbie and Ken wandering around. I was pleased Robbie had come so promptly. Now we were aware of the school's shortcomings, it was imperative to set things right as soon as we could.

Robbie was there all morning,

assessing the situation. He opened the screen door of my classroom as I was arranging texts for the next period. There were only the two of us.

'G'day.' He hovered by the door, reticent to enter without permission.

'Hello,' I replied, coolly. After our last meeting, I was concerned about saying the wrong thing. 'Come on in. Close the screen. I can do without any more flies.'

'Sorry. Heard about your heroics. You were a right little ripper. Didn't think you had it in you.'

'Why — because I'm a woman?' My hackles were raised and he had only just entered!

'Lord, no! I just thought you were the sort to sit back and watch, that's all. You proved me wrong. Guess I'm not a good judge of character. No offence.' He paused, staring at the boots on his feet. 'I'll examine the alarm and clear off. Don't want to hold you up.' He took a few steps towards the smashed glass over the alarm button. 'Oh, and ta for putting my name up for doing this. Appreciate any work these days.'

It was a genuine thanks. Putting my text books down I went to stand near him. 'What's the verdict then? Why didn't the alarm sound?'

'Here, Debra. I'll show you.' Taking a screwdriver from his work-belt, he undid the four screws holding the box in place then lifted it off. It was clear what the problem was.

'No wires? It's not connected, is it?' I was absolutely astounded. 'That's criminal!'

'Same with all the other alarms, bar one. Whoever fitted these was a right drongo.'

It was obvious now. 'The one that was tested after installation,' I surmised. Student lives had been in danger from the day the complex system had first been installed. These fire alarms were as much use as an ashtray on a motorbike!

'I've already notified the authorities in Hobart. They'll send their own inspector this arvo. All these alarms on the walls are simply for show — empty promises of safety, garbage. And I agree with you — it's criminal. I'll do an estimate to fix the system and give it to Ken before I go. Won't be cheap, though.'

'Can you give me an idea?'

He weighed it up, referring to his notes. 'Won't see much change from a grand.'

I whistled. Almost two months wages for me. 'It needs doing, though. Thanks for coming out so quickly.'

He shrugged his shoulders. 'Not much else on. Like I told you, Debra. I'm not a popular bloke around here. Thought you would have heard about that by now.'

I stared into his eyes. There was a tenderness there that surprised me, given his rugged, muscular build. But as I'd learned with Shane, appearances weren't reliable for showing the real person inside.

'I make my own decisions about people, Robbie. I'm not one for gossip

— and my apologies for being awkward when you came in. I'm a bit vulnerable myself . . . man trouble. I'd like to be your friend, though.'

Extending a hand to shake his was an unusual gesture for most women but I had my own way of doing things. Robbie hesitated a second before clasping my hand in his. Talk about strong!

'Friends,' I said, with a genuine smile.

'Yeah, definitely.'

'Before you go, can I have a word or two about the situation regarding these alarms?'

'Sure. I brought some literature with me — reference material and such. I have a good idea about these things but we have to follow very exacting rules. What do you want to find out?'

★　★　★

Lunchtime came and went. As I'd not been on playground duty, I'd suggested to Tom that he could come for more remedial work. He was very pleased.

When the time came, two others from my 1A class asked if they could join.

'Pleased to have you here,' I told them as we settled down to some intensive work. That Remedial English course I'd done at Uni was paying off.

'Can we come tomorrow lunch, Miss?' one of them asked, a definite eagerness in her voice.

'I'm afraid not. I'm on playground duty. How about after school?'

Sad faces told me they were bus students, so lunch was the only time.

It was a great rewarding day overall. I was keen to check on the latest about the fire so visited Ken's office after the children had been dismissed for the day and were on their way home.

Knocking on the headmaster's door, I was greeted by a less than enthusiastic, 'Come in.'

Ken's face was sullen, as was the way he was slumped in his chair. 'Debra.' He motioned for me to take a seat.

'You look like you could use a choccie pick-me-up.'

'Way past that, I'm afraid. That Robbie bloke showed me the fiasco of our so-called alarm system and I sent his quote off by fax. Just heard back. They're not going to fund it for at least two months. Damned pen-pushers!'

I was flabbergasted. 'But they can't do that.'

'They can and they have,' Ken replied, resting his head on his open hands, elbows on his desk. He was very despondent.

'No. I mean it — they can't do that, legally.'

He sat back, swept his dishevelled hair off his forehead and asked me to explain.

'Better than that, I'll talk to them.' He seemed sceptical, so I persisted. 'I can't make it any worse, can I?'

'Well, actually you could. You're not the most diplomatic of people.' He gave me a wan look.

I grinned. 'I know. And that's exactly why you need me. My middle names are Be Prepared.'

I removed a thick folder from my case and opened it at the bookmarked page which Robbie had shown me. Ken started to read, the frown on his leathery face quickly changing to a smile.

5

Ken dialled the department that over-saw school's budgets and passed the phone to me. One of the new features on the telephone Commander system he was using was a loud speaker so more than one person could listen in. I asked for the individual who had made the decision to postpone any repairs.

'I'm sorry, ma'am. He's busy right now. Perhaps you should phone back on Monday?'

I suspected Mr McGavin was getting ready to leave for the weekend. One thing I'd learned about officials was that their weekend started well before the usual finishing time of five on a Friday. Maybe he had a date with a golf putter.

'My name is Debra Winters. I'm from All Saints High. I assure you, he'll want to talk to me.'

As we waited, I put my hand over the

mouthpiece. 'See, boss — I can be diplomatic.'

Within seconds a very pompous Mr McGavin's voice echoed through the Headmaster's office.

'What do you want, Miss . . . Winters? I've told your principal that we can't release funds for the Fire Alarms. I'm a very busy man.'

'I appreciate that, Mr McGavin. You'll soon be a very famous man too.'

That caught him off guard. 'Famous?'

'Because of your decision the school will have to close. Imagine all of those kiddies' parents ringing you up because you were too stingy to fix the safety systems which, according to Tasmanian Government Law 47, Bylaw 16, Paragraph XV, must be installed and functioning in all schools in the state — and I quote, 'Failure to do so will result in the immediate closure of said institution.' Unquote.'

There was a lengthy pause. 'And why should I listen to you? You're only a teacher.'

'Because I'll tell the papers. Or have you forgotten the name of the Editor-in-chief of the Mercury — Sebastian Winters.'

'Winters? Don't tell me you're related to him.' There was a touch of panic in his voice.

'Would it make a difference if I were? Please advise us that the monies are in the All Saints building account within . . . oh, let's say, an hour. After that, I'll be on the phone to my uncle. Thanks very much. Goodbye, Mr McGavin.'

I disconnected the call, sat back in my chair and took a long, deep breath. 'I think I need one of those Cherry Ripes now, please Ken.'

He quickly obliged. 'You never told me your uncle was editor of the Mercury.'

I took a well-earned bite. 'He isn't. He's a bus driver in Launceston. I ring him once a week. You don't mind me calling later, do you? Wouldn't want to be branded a liar.' I gave my boss a wink.

Ken burst out laughing just as a fax came through. We read it together. The funds were in the account. He reached out to shake my hand, before sitting down to ring Robbie, who had been awaiting news at home. An early start tomorrow morning was agreed. Clearly, as he'd told me, the Fire Chief didn't have much other work scheduled.

It was then that Ken admitted he was impressed with my negotiation skills. 'You've done this sort of thing before, Miss Winters?'

'Once or twice. I don't like men talking down to me. I spent a lot of time in my father's office up in Launceston during school hols. My mother passed away when I was eight. I learned a lot about dealing with people, especially bureaucrats. He's retired from doctoring now but those life lessons paid off.'

'Your dad would be proud of you. I'd like to meet him, Debra.'

'Perhaps you will, Ken. He's coming down to visit in a month's time.'

After Tuesday morning's staff briefing, Ken called me aside to say he'd take my lunchtime playground duties so I could make my remedial classes a regular event for those First Formers who wanted to attend. Of course, I wasn't obliged to do them, but he wanted to support me if I wished to continue.

'You don't have to do that,' I protested.

'I do, actually. I'll explain one day. Robbie will fit a temporary system to all rooms starting today so that we have our safety net ASAP. The permanent ones will take longer, obviously.'

My teaching day was quite hectic so I didn't have a chance to speak to Robbie although he popped into my lessons from time to time, attaching covered wiring he'd dropped from the roof void. Later, Robbie was in the parking lot, putting materials into his station wagon when I made my way up to the back road with my Roll-Call class after school finished. Most of the other pupils were already lined up at their respective buses. Robbie turned to wave before heading back to the school buildings.

It only took a few minutes then that was it. The kids were all gone, collected by parents or on their bus, heading home. I was finished for the day too. I had my case and bag with me already so I could go straight to the parking lot. It was time for that visit to the real estate agents to check on local accommodation. I wasn't hopeful.

Despite being in the shade, I had to wind the windows down before starting Lulu. Choke out, gear in neutral, hand-brake on. Turning the ignition key, all that happened was a clunk. Not good. I tried again. Was the battery flat? Exasperated, I got out to open the bonnet before realising I didn't have a clue what to look for. Then I saw Robbie returning to his van with more boxes.

'Robbie. I have a car problem. Can you help?'

'Sure, Teach, if I can. What's wrong?'

'Lulu won't start. Battery?' He grinned at me calling my car by a name. I guessed it was a lady thing to do.

He jumped in, his lanky frame cramped up in the front seat. Another clunk. He then turned the lights on and I reported back they were working.

'Not the battery then,' he said. 'Starter motor? Yeah, I reckon it's that. Just phone the RACT and they'll sort it.'

I hit myself on the head. Dumb bunny Debra. Why didn't I think of that? Opening my handbag, I reached in to retrieve my membership card and was about to head off to the main office to ring when I noticed the expiry date.

'Oh, no! It ran out, end of last month. I must have forgotten to renew it. You sure it's the starter motor, Robbie? Can't you just jump start it or push it down a hill or something?' I was getting angry. After all, I'd promised Lulu I'd take her to a garage for a check-up last Saturday but, with the fire and all, it hadn't happened.

He looked at the perfectly flat area where my car was parked. 'No. 'Fraid not.'

'What am I going to do?' I retrieved my bags from the back seat and dumped them, unceremoniously on the Tarmac, giving one tyre a decent kick. Hobart was too far for a taxi, there were no buses going that way and no one I knew was driving there any time soon. Not to put too fine a point on it, but I was totally stuffed.

'You OK there Debra?' Robbie asked.

'No, I'm not,' I replied a little too loudly, instantly regretting my temper.

'Perhaps I can help sort you out,' Robbie said.

'What? Offer me an overnight stay at your place? I don't think so, Mr Sanderson.'

'You do like to jump in feet first, Miss Winters. Typical Aries, as my sister would say. You're a right little firestorm. No, not my place. I was thinking of you staying at my sister's home up near

Huonville. As for that car of yours, I have a mechanic mate in the garage down the road who can fix it. Won't be today, though.'

Well that was embarrassing. Was I usually this tetchy? Maybe it was the heat but that was just an excuse. The problem was me.

'Sorry, Robbie. Short temper syndrome. I wish I could be as calm as you are.' The two of us went off to the main office where the phone was.

Robbie asked Mrs Alliprandi if he could use the office phone. 'Two private calls, please.' He paid her and spoke for a few minutes while I stood outside in the shade, still fuming at myself for being so upset.

Robbie appeared. 'All sorted out. Only problem for you is accepting a lift from yours truly to get to my sister's. I can take you in about an hour when I knock off here. Or you can always walk.'

Walking wasn't an option — not in this heat. On the other hand, waiting around wasn't ideal but Robbie had his own important work to do here.

'A lift would be much appreciated. I can help you out in the meantime if you like, passing stuff and fetching. Least I can do for being — '

'A right little madam?' He laughed. It was one of those deep, genuine and unrestrained laughs. This Robbie wasn't the sort of bloke to be afraid to express himself. 'Yeah. A helping hand'd be groovy. Ta muchly.'

He indicated the store room where the electric junction box was. Perhaps I'd let him know that 'groovy' was well out of date for modern slang. Or perhaps not. After all, what harm was it doing?

We didn't talk much in that hour. OK, there were lots of sentences like, 'Fetch me those red cutters' but, like most men, he could only concentrate on one thing at a time. He completed connecting the temporary alarms from one side of the play area and, one by one, we tried them. Ken was there to check.

By the time we were finished, it was closer to two hours, although I didn't mind. Watching those large hands of his teasing tiny wires into even tinier gaps was fascinating and therapeutic at the same time. It was evident he had a gift for electrics, newly qualified or not.

His station wagon had seen better days, for sure. Gallantly, he opened my door for me then hastily spread a relatively clean blanket over the dusty bench seat on my side. I stepped in and wound the window down. It had been parked in the shade but was still hot inside.

We were half way to Huonville, passing pleasantries about nothing much, when I decided to do a bit of detective work. We hadn't talked about him or his big sister at all. I began, 'I appreciate how you helped out back there, even though you didn't need to, Robbie.'

His eyes were fixed on the road, even though the traffic was almost non-existent. His blond hair was ruffled by the warm wind through the open window. 'I owed you, since you suggested my name for that job.'

That was disappointing. So much for a knight in khaki shorts, dashing to my rescue!

'Sorry about being angry back there. That's not the real me. Honest. These past few weeks have been difficult. I had a boyfriend up in Hobart. He and I taught in the same school and we had plans to get married — until I discovered he was having an affair with the headmaster's wife.' I paused. It was hard to talk about it without breaking into tears or hitting something. 'At first, he denied it but one of my friends had photographed them kissing. That's when I left him — two weeks ago. Now he wants me back . . . and me to go back to my old school.'

Robbie glanced at me. Though his sunnies masked his reaction, I detected shock there. 'It'd be terrible if you left All Saints. The kids love you. At least, that's what my niece says.'

It was an over-reaction if he were

simply concerned about the kids, I thought. 'I'm not going, Robbie. Shane and I are history.'

That calmed him. He drove in silence for a short distance, then I went on, 'Also, he stole all my money, the lying rat. I hate him, really hate him,' I blurted out for no reason before feeling tears in my eyes. Hastily I leaned forward against the seat belt to retrieve a hanky from my handbag. A peek in the sun visor mirror showed my eyes were red. I dabbed them carefully. 'Sorry,' I mumbled between sobs.

'Don't be. From the sounds of it, I figure you've had a rough few weeks. And I'm glad you're not thinking of leaving. Crikey, we only just became friends, Debra. And I haven't got many of those, 'cept for Jimmy.'

OK, as confessions to a virtual stranger went, that had gone further than I'd intended. Robbie must reckon I was a cry-baby. All of a sudden, my life had been turned upside down, Shane had taken all that I'd had apart from my little car.

The road sign read *Huonville 5km*. 'Can we stop at a shop, please? I need a few essentials like a toothbrush.'

'Sure. Wendy says you can borrow one of her nighties,' he replied.

'Thanks.' I didn't think it was appropriate to mention I slept in the nude.

'Debra. There's something you need to be told about me. The reason people round here don't think much of me. You deserve to know the truth.'

I reached over to touch his hand on the steering wheel. 'Like I said, Robbie, I make my own decisions about people. I'll still like you.'

'We'll see . . . well, ten or more years ago, I was a right little larrikin . . . fighting, drinking, you name it. Got me a bit of a reputation in The Valley. My dad had gone walkabout when I was a nipper and my mum, bless her soul, she couldn't deal with me. Nicked a car or two just to ride around in but I never went to jail. I was lucky that two blokes turned my life around.' He was clearly uncomfortable telling me this. Aussie men weren't great for sharing emotions.

'It's OK, Robbie. That's who you were, not who you are now. Was this Jimmy one of the men?'

We were alongside the river now. 'Yeah. Good old Jimmy. Got me into the Fire Brigade. Showed me there was more to life. These days I stay out of trouble. Some blokes reckon I'm a bit of a coward because of that but I'm not bothered. If it came to it, I could handle myself in a fight but that's not my style. Not any more.'

He sighed, slowing down as we came into the town's speed limit zone. We pulled up on the main street near the movie theatre. I went off by myself while Robbie wandered down to the newsagents to get a paper and have a browse. He didn't lock the car though; the difference between city and country living, I guessed. Even so, I kept an eye on it from inside the refreshingly cool shop.

It wasn't long before we set off again. Robbie was more relaxed as we crossed the bridge over the Huon and turned right towards the Glen Huon Valley where the river began. I'd heard of it, but living in the north of Tassie until I began Uni, I'd never visited it. According to Robbie, there was a road either side of the river, meeting at Glen Huon some ten kilometres up the road.

The steep wooded slopes towered above us as we wove past the occasional house made of weatherboard with 'tin' roofs. The roofs were actually corrugated iron coated in zinc to stop them rusting.

'I'll give you a lift back tomorrow and give your keys to my mechanic mate. He'll sort you out, and won't rip you off either. Is eight o'clock OK?'

I said it was. I'd actually be at school early for a change.

'My place is a bit further along. Used to be Mum's but she's dead now. Left it to me. Wendy has her own place with Heather and Chris. Mine's pretty run

103

down. You'll like Wendy. Used to be a science teacher, mainly biology. These days she manages the farm.'

'A teacher, eh?'

Robbie swerved suddenly to avoid a stupid Echidna taking his time to cross the road. It was more dangerous to drive at night because a lot of our native critters were nocturnal.

'And Heather is in one of your classes.'

'Heather Powell?' In my lovely first form class, she was well-mannered and bright, as well as being mature for her age. It always struck me as a little strange that girls often matured faster than boys both physically and mentally.

'It's just up here on the next road left. Wendy has it decorated well. If you saw my place, you'd probably think it hadn't been lived in for ages.'

In front of us, the southern slope of the valley soared skyward. Trees covered the hillside. Wendy's farm wasn't as brown as elsewhere. I saw a sprinkler on the gardens along the drive to the house.

'There's an artesian spring they use for watering plants and livestock. Wendy's garden's like a little oasis. There she is, under the porch.'

A woman wearing a bright yellow dress waved. She wore glasses with medium length blonde hair framing her welcoming face.

We pulled up next to an old Falcon that had been two-tone before the brown dust covering.

'G'day, you two. Come on in. I'm Wendy, and you must be Debbie.' I noticed Robbie and her grinning at some mysterious joke.

'I prefer Debra, thanks.'

She smiled. 'Very pleased to meet you, Debra.' Wendy ushered me in past the fly-screen door while Robbie grabbed my school case.

The inside was dark and cool, a welcome relief from the afternoon sun. The baby-pink venetian blinds were all closed. There was a long gallery with table and chairs opposite the kitchen. The rest of the gallery was narrower leading down to a room with a large and comfy looking armchair.

The odour of lamb cooking filled the air.

'Have a seat, you two. Cold drink? Lemonade or perhaps a beer? Not for Robbie of course . . . ' She was talking ten to the dozen, clearly nervous to make a good impression.

Robbie put his hand on his sister's shoulder.

'Crikey, Wendy. Give the kid a chance.' He laughed. 'Wendy here doesn't get to entertain much. It'll be good for her to have you to chinwag with, even if it is only for one night.'

'A lemonade will be fine,' I said, graciously. My mouth was dry, probably from all the chatter in the car.

Wendy put her apron on and went to the oven to check on the lamb, then to the large fridge. Robbie and I took a seat. After giving us our drinks, she put two more glasses on the large sassafras table.

'Excuse me,' she said, going towards

the lounge. 'Heather, finish up your homework and join us for a drink.'

My student appeared, freshly changed from her uniform into jeans and a checked cotton shirt. She was quite the young lady, her frizzy hair nothing like her mum's.

'Hiya, Miss Winters.' Her voice was effervescent. She was clearly not intimidated by her teacher being here.

'Hello, Heather. I hope me staying here tonight isn't a problem for you.'

'No, it's cool, Miss Winters.' She sat and we all had a drink.

Turning to Wendy, I thanked her for coming to the rescue, offering to pay for my overnight stay.

'Wouldn't hear of it. Think of it as a welcome to The Valley pressie.'

Once we finished our drinks, Wendy showed me to my room. It was quite spacious with a large glass door opening onto the veranda and the shade of two large magnolia trees. The dirt driveway was just the other side.

'Bathroom's down there. We usually

shower in the evening. Does morning suit you?'

It did. When I offered to help prepare dinner, Wendy told me it was in hand, so I settled down in my comfy room to do some marking and preparation for a drama lesson tomorrow. There was an old padded armchair that was great to flop down in. The bed had an eiderdown cover with a nightie neatly folded on it. I'd probably use it, given the presence of a man in the house and the possibility Heather might see me.

After an hour or so doing school work, I decided a stroll outside before tea was in order. The freshly-cut cerise chrysanthemums had such an engaging, heady scent, I was eager to find out what other delights were out there. Exiting through my outside door, I passed from the cool of the magnolias to the sunlit garden surrounding the house. There was a mixture of Australian natives along with conventional European plants like azaleas and pelargoniums. The Aussie ones included bottlebrush, kangaroo paw and a waratah. There were also dozens of mauve and white agapanthus which originally weren't Australian but were now a part of our landscape. Like our human population, the gardens were a melange of plants from all over.

In the distance, I could hear a car approaching. There was a cloud of dust too. Before I realised it, a police car was there, stopping outside the sprawling homestead. An officer stepped out of the car, his back to me as he reached inside the vehicle. Who was he after? Who knew I was here?

When he turned around, he spied me standing there on the veranda. 'Miss Winters? Good. I wanted a word with you.'

6

Once he took off his sunglasses and cap, I recognised him straight away. 'Senior Sergeant. What are you doing here?'

He grinned an uncharacteristic grin for a policeman. 'I live here.'

It took a moment before I thumped my forehead with the heel of my hand. Stupid me! 'You're Chris Powell. My apologies. My brain must be on walkabout today.' The blue shirts on the clothes line plus other little clues suddenly made sense. 'You said you wanted a word?'

'Yeah. Wendy phoned the station, told me you were staying with us. Just wanted to tell you how pleased we are to have you here, at least for the night.'

It was a strange way to finish his statement, I thought, but it was a relief. 'I'm just admiring Wendy's green fingers.' I indicated the garden.

'She has a veggie patch out back, too.' Chris glanced at his watch. 'Tea time. You ready?'

'You bet,' I replied, joining him as he walked to the front door. If there weren't the constant concern about the threat of bushfires, this sort of weather was idyllic for a sun-lover like me.

'I've got some news for you about your junior firebug, but it can wait until later.'

As we entered it was great to witness the love in this household. Heather ran up to give her dad a huge hug, Wendy joining in too.

'Where's Robbie?' I asked, not seeing him.

Wendy disengaged herself from Chris's arms. 'He's gone, Debra, although I did ask him to stay for tea. He went to see how his friend is. Jimmy's not been well for a while.'

There was a surreptitious glance between Wendy and Chris.

'Oh, OK.' I was disappointed for

some reason. Perhaps it was because I thought we'd connected in some meaningful way.

'He said he'd pick you up tomorrow, though,' Wendy added. That brought an unexpected smile from me. If Wendy noticed, she said nothing.

★ ★ ★

I asked permission to ring Carrie-Anne. She'd be home by now. The explanation was no surprise to her. 'I kept telling you to get that car of yours checked out properly, Debra. Sounds like you were lucky with the accommodation.'

'Yes. They seem to be a lovely family.' No one was around so I wasn't saying it for their benefit.

'And what about your fireman friend?'

'He's been quite helpful. Good-looking too, like that helicopter pilot in *Skippy*. Strangely he does seem ill-at-ease around me. Am I that scary?'

Carrie-Anne laughed. 'Hardly, Debra. Surely, you're not thinking of being more than friends though. You only just finished with him whose name should not be mentioned.'

'No, just friends, I'm a fire sign and he's a water one, not a good combination according to astrology — or so I'm told. Romance is not on the cards — or in the stars.'

'I'm a water sign and we get on fine. Anyway, since when did you start believing in astrology?'

'I don't. It just came up in a conversation with him. He doesn't believe in it either. I'd best go now — tea's almost ready. See you tomorrow night, babe. Hope you won't be too lonely.'

The meal was sumptuous — leg of lamb, with butternut pumpkin, peas and squash as well as the obligatory roast potatoes. However, it was the warmth and genuine joy that struck me as the thing I most enjoyed. Heather joined in freely, showing none of the shyness I usually associated with students her age as they began adolescence.

After washing up we all moved to the

lounge area where we enjoyed bowls of Neapolitan ice-cream. The telly was there but remained switched off as each of us relaxed. It felt totally bizarre to kick my shoes off and unwind with people who had been, and still were, strangers. I imagined it was weirder for them, opening up their home to someone they had no idea about. Would I be an untidy slob, not cleaning up after myself? Would I be rude or anti-social? It would be a learning curve, much more so than sharing a dorm in Uni. At least there us girls had been in the same boat.

Initially, I was mindful of the presence of Heather. I'd never mixed socially with a pupil I taught before, always believing there should be some distance between me and those I taught. Getting too close would make me vulner-able to gossip. In the small-town community around All Saints that could scupper whatever authority and respect I had.

It was Wendy who inquired about why I'd chosen to teach locally. I must

114

have shifted uncomfortably in my armchair because Chris spoke up.

'Debra, you're apprehensive about discussing personal things in front of Heather, here. Understandable.' He held his hand out to his daughter. 'But Heather learned from an early age never to talk about what we disclose here. Remember, I'm a copper. When Wendy asks me about work, I answer her. She's made loads of suggestions over the years. And Wendy was a teacher once, down at your school.'

'You were?' That was a surprise.

Wendy replied. 'I was a part time science teacher until the numbers dropped and they cut back on staff. Naturally Martin Day stayed. He's been there forever.'

'No stories were ever spread by Heather. She's our precious girl and we've always shared everything with her.'

'So, I can trust you, Heather?' She nodded. 'I'm not comfortable about this but I'm going to let you in on some secrets about me. Not even your bestest friend can be told.' I took a deep breath. Outside the setting sun gave the room a warm rosy glow. 'I broke up with my boyfriend, Shane. He cheated on me. But because he taught in the same school as me, I had to move. We were getting married, too.' Even thinking about his betrayal still hurt and I was getting upset. Without thinking, I described how I felt about him and his betrayal of all that I'd believed we had, using a swear word. Immediately, I apologised for my language.

Chris sat forward, his manner radiating anger and concern. 'If that's what this Shane bloke did, you've no need to apologise. I'm ashamed to admit Heather's heard far worse from me.'

Wendy spoke up. 'Robbie mentioned that he stole money from your joint account.'

Normally, I would have been reticent to air my dirty laundry, yet here, with this family, it somehow felt cathartic. The only other person I'd shared this with was Carrie-Anne, not even my dad.

'Yeah. Forged my signature, I think.'

Chris kicked into policeman mode. 'If you care to make a formal complaint, Debra . . . ?'

'Not right now. I need to contact the bank first.'

Chris replied, 'They'll only refer it to us. Hobart branch have specialists who deal with this.'

'I'll see. Things are very raw between Shane and me right now,' I confessed.

Chris sat back ruffling his dark brown hair. 'I can't imagine how you must feel. New job, new home, and no one to support you. Even though you seem to be a strong, independent young lady, we're here for you now. All of us. Right, team?'

The two others echoed Chris's genuine sentiments. I recalled how he'd been when we'd first met on the highway, brightening my day up with his much-needed pep talk.

However, Heather was the one who

117

made me realise just how supportive this family were to one another — and now to me. 'It's not your fault, Miss Winters. All you were guilty of was believing in a man who never deserved your love.' Then she came over to give me a hug, which I returned.

Wendy spoke next, reaching out to Chris. This was what a true loving relationship should be. What Shane and I had was nowhere as meaningful as what was here in this room.

'That explains a lot, Debra. That journey to and from Hobart isn't ideal either.'

'I'm searching for a place to stay in The Valley. I've had no luck yet and where I'm staying in Hobart . . . well, it's a temporary fix.'

'That's what I reckoned.' Wendy was stroking the cat on her lap, although she was facing me. She took off her glasses to clean them with the hem of her dress. She had such a kind face. 'When Robbie asked if you could stay here tonight, it got me thinking . . . I

118

checked with Chris and Heather and we all think it would be a great idea. What we've seen of you tonight confirms it. Would you consider boarding here with us? We'd understand if you said no . . . '

I had no problem living with a family. It would be better than being on my own, brooding. And it wasn't as though I had any love life. The very personal conversation we'd just had made sense now — they'd decided to ask me to stay already; I wasn't just an overnight visitor. From what I'd seen, we'd all get on just fine together. I had a good feeling about this.

'That would be absolutely wonderful,' I said.

We discussed some practicalities, settling on me paying twenty-five dollars a week half-board. I'd have the room I was currently in, starting Thursday. That way I could return to Carrie-Anne's tomorrow night to get some of my possessions, and collect the rest on the weekend.

It was now my turn to pick Chris's brains. What had happened about the arson attempt at the school?

'We caught up with Freddie without too much hassle. Don't even need your witness testimony. His prints were everywhere and he was still wearing his paint-covered clothes when we picked him up. After showing him the evidence, he owned up. He won't be setting any more fires for a while.'

That was a relief for me and, I thought, my fellow teachers at All Saints.

'How do you feel about that, Heather?' I asked.

'Good. No one likes him, Miss Winters.' She was honest and not afraid of speaking her mind. I guessed her strong mum and dad had a great deal to do with that attitude.

'And what about closing the door on me? Did he own up to that?' I asked Chris.

He grinned a little sheepishly. 'No. Said he'd scarpered when he realised he'd been seen. Our fire investigator found the problem, though. The lock on the hydraulic closing piston was faulty. I'm guessing you assumed it would keep the door ajar, but it didn't.'

That was a sobering thought. Those books on the floor were just a precaution as the door was already open, but they weren't strong enough to prevent it closing when the piston lock failed. If it hadn't been for Doris and Ken . . .

★ ★ ★

During the drive to school with Robbie, I was a different person. Solving the accommodation problem was a weight off my mind. Although Heather had been offered a lift too, she told Robbie she preferred the bus with her friends. It was understandable. Being seen arriving with a teacher was not cool at all, no matter who the teacher was.

'You seem chirpier this morning, Debra. Anything you'd like to tell me?'

'I reckon you can guess, Robbie, as I

121

suspect you had a hand in it. I'll be staying at the Powells' for the foreseeable future. They're a lovely family.'

'Yes. Totally agree with you, though I am a bit prejudiced. Wendy was considering asking you to board there so I just gave things a bit of a nudge when I saw you had a transport problem.'

The morning was quite cool from the clear night and the forecast was for a more temperate week which was good — less chance of fires. Not that Robbie was on call for a few days, according to Wendy. Then I remembered . . .

'There's something that might brighten your day, too, Mr Sanderson — Chris informed us that there are quite a few repercussions from the school alarm fiasco.'

Robbie turned his head slightly towards me, his sunglasses masking his emotions.

'Go on, Miss Schoolteacher. Don't keep me in suspenders.' We grinned at his little joke.

'That Sammy O'Rourke who fitted the alarm has been banned from doing any more work — his permission's been

122

cancelled. An EPL, I think.'

Robbie explained. 'Electrical Practitioner's Licence. That's good news. Once people hear he can't do any electrics, there'll be more work for me. Word of mouth is important around here and the council have already signed me up.'

Council? That prompted a recollection of something else that Chris had said last night.

'The guy from the council's in big trouble, too. He OK-ed the work as conforming to regulations. He'd already left under a cloud but now he's up for corruption charges, taking back-handers.'

'Never did like the guy. Can't say I'm upset to see him get his come-uppance. He tried asking me for money to pass a building job once.'

'Are there a lot of bent people in the Huon?'

'Course not. Most are fine, law-abiding people. But considering the Huon Valley is the apple-growing centre of Australia, you've got to expect a few rotten apples in the population.'

I gave him a little clap. 'Rotten apples? Very clever, Mr Sanderson.'

We had the windows open just a little as there was some dust around from the arid landscape. A decent rain was long overdue. Tassie was a real enigma rain-wise. Tullah on the west coast had close to three metres per year — four times as much as Huonville and eight times as much as Ross in the Midlands.

A flock of sulphur-crested cockatoos wheeled by in front of the car, screeching their good morning greeting. It was a different world out here compared to the city of Hobart. Tassie was a beautiful state. It was a pity so few other Aussies visited.

'Did you catch up with your mate, Jimmy?'

'I did. For all the good it did. He's not the man I knew.' He was concerned for his friend, judging by his voice. No, concerned was the wrong word . . . more disappointed.

'Care to elaborate, Robbie?'

'Not really. Not right now, anyway.

Let's just say he was once the sort of bloke you could look up to and admire. These days he's a shadow of his former self. Drinks and gambles far too much.'

'That's sad. Yet you visit him nevertheless.'

'Only to check he's OK. Had a row last night, though. He threw me out.'

'Tell me if I'm prying too much, Robbie. What was the row about?'

'Believe it or not it was about the new casino at Wrest Point. Difference of opinion about places like that. Let's drop it now. We need to discuss sorting this car of yours out.'

'OK. Whatever you want.'

Once again, he'd closed me down when I was offering to listen. Maybe one day I'd break through that crusty exterior of his . . . although I sensed it would be far from easy.

★ ★ ★

The most frustrating aspect that I found in teaching was the lack of tangible results at the end of each day. By tangible, I meant an object that one might touch and say, 'Hey, everyone. See what I made today'. Teachers weren't carpenters, or electricians like Robbie, or stockbrokers who could declare how much money they'd made when they went home to their wives or hubbies.

Our results were imparting skills and knowledge that might be assessed with some exam in the future, even if it wasn't the whole picture. Apart from teaching my pupils to appreciate literature and poetry, my aim was to teach them how to keep learning, how to interact with others, to grow into adulthood with positive values. And if they had some fun acting in a play in my classroom, that was a great result too.

My lunchtime remedial sessions had five students, all keen to learn. Already I saw so much improvement in their reading. In place of the monotonous sameness of their voices as they struggled with each word, they were putting phrases, together, pausing at commas, raising their tone at question marks. It was the confidence that shone through — and it was contagious.

'Mum was dead impressed when I read my poems last night, Miss Winters.'

'Please use 'very' instead of 'dead', Tom — but I'm happy to hear that.'

Outside the window I saw Ken doing my playground duty. As I took a dainty bite of a Violet Crumble bar, I wondered why he felt obliged to help me out. It was simply another paradox about his behaviour.

From time to time, Robbie popped into my room throughout the day, messing with wires and tools. It was a large job for one person. He'd nod or say 'Hi' before disappearing up a ladder into the roof void.

Then one time he explained my car was all fixed before giving me my keys back.

'You can pay Colin next week if you want. Here's his bill, plus a detailed account.'

As I was free the last period of the day, I decided to visit and pay Colin as well as checking if my bank account had been transferred from Hobart to here. It was so inconvenient because the bank was open only from ten to three o'clock. How normal working people were meant to deposit or withdraw money had always been a mystery. It was as though the banks thought they were doing us a favour by deigning to open at all. I still had my last pay cheque in my handbag and though I could pay Colin with a cheque, my cash was running low.

Meeting Colin was an experience. His laugh was infectious and very, very loud. His garage was busy with two mechanics working on tractors, trucks and even that 1960s yellow Vauxhall Victor I'd seen a woman using to collect a boy from school each day.

Walking down the main street with its half dozen shops, I felt as though everyone was staring at me. Well they would, I decided. I was, like that Del

Shannon song, a *Stranger In Town*. A few recognised me as the new teacher, the gentlemen tipping their wide-brimmed hats and saying my name. I gathered some of the local women disapproved of the length of my dress but that was their problem, not mine.

Tassie was about to change, whether some people liked it or not. Our state had been hit hard when Britain joined up with European countries in their new trading arrangements. Suddenly our apple producers had lost a large portion of their market. There was some resentment but, more than that, the realisation that we needed money from elsewhere and tourism was now being regarded as the panacea for our ailing economy.

Until now, there was no reason for mainlanders from the rest of Australia to visit Tassie. They could see our unique wildlife in zoos, so why cross the Bass Strait to come here? After all, many of them believed that our state was only full of trees and backward people!

The annual Sydney to Hobart yacht

race had started in 1945 and attracted a lot of reporters and TV news crews to the big finish in Constitution Dock around New Year. Quite a few spectators too. However, they stayed and spent their money for one week, if that. No one came for the rest of the year.

That was all about to change. Tassie had voted by a referendum to allow a casino to be opened in our state. As none of the other five states had anything like it, Hobart would be the place to go for Australia's high-rollers. At least, that was the plan — and the reason I'd voted for it. Those more affluent people would spend money elsewhere in Hobart or touring our isle, and that would boost our flagging economy.

Wrest Point Casino was a cylindrical tower of seventeen storeys on the bank of the beautiful Derwent River. In addition to the casino it had a hotel, shops and restaurants, including a revolving one on the top floor. And it was, now open. Our very own tourist attraction, for the rich and those who aspired to win money while dressed in their Sunday best. If they saw a famous footie player or a big-name TV or movie star, all the better.

I was planning to go there for the buffet lunch on Saturday and to have a squizz at what it had to offer. The evenings would be much busier and the longer it was open, the more word of mouth should assist in boosting our state's economy.

Of course, not everyone approved. The referendum had been close. Robbie had already voiced his disapproval and while I respected all opinions, that was one thing my new friend and I would never agree on.

★ ★ ★

Following my final night's stay with Carrie-Anne, I packed as much as I could into my small car and set off for my next adventure. It would be hard sharing my life with a family. When

Mum passed away, there had just been Dad and me. It was never ideal given Dad's work commitments but I had to admit there was a lot of love and support.

I'd moved down from Launceston to attend the University of Tasmania, living in dormitories with Carrie-Anne and others. After that, a few years renting by myself before giving that up to move in with that slug, Shane. Naturally, I'd not thought of him as a slug back then.

I stayed after school for an hour or so, preparing and marking. Robbie was not around, although we did now have functioning temporary alarms throughout the school. He had other work that he'd delayed to prioritise us. Saying that, he'd told Ken he'd be back tomorrow.

It was my plan to spend the time after I arrived at the Powells', helping Wendy and having a proper talk. Putting my precious possessions away could wait until the weekend. Finding my way there was a bit of guesswork, because I hadn't taken a great deal of notice when Robbie had driven. Wendy was waiting with some cool drinks when I eventually arrived. I plopped the cases and few boxes in my room. It felt good to have this place so much closer to my new school.

When I entered the long gallery kitchen, Wendy was just hanging up the phone. She removed her glasses to rub her eyes, her normally vibrant, cheery features now worried. At that moment, there was a loud noise above the ceiling in the roof loft. Wendy ignored it as if it was quite normal yet the cat stared upwards, mildly intrigued.

'What's that racket?' I wondered.

'Nothing. Possum playtime. One day I'll have to get them out properly but they're so clever, I've taken pity on them. Those paws of theirs have beaten me every time I've nailed the gaps in the roof closed. It's as if they insist it's their home too and no pesky human with a hammer is going to stop them from squatting up there.'

Possums were nocturnal. They'd play around outside at night using their big eyes to see with, eating fruit they'd hold in their paws. Often their young would be there, clinging to their back when they were too large for Mum's pouch.

'They're not the problem, are they?' was my question, understanding that it wasn't as simple as mad marsupials cavorting in the loft.

Wendy sighed, nodding to the phone. 'That was Chris. Told me the same thing as Robbie did twenty minutes ago. A lot of these fires plaguing Tassie don't make sense. There's been few lightning strikes and they start well away from frequented areas like picnic spots where some drongo left his barbie still alight.'

She put her glasses back on then stared at me with concern etched on the tanned face. 'They have proof. There's an arsonist loose — and it seems he intends to incinerate our bush.'

7

Astonished that anyone could be that evil, I asked, 'Are they absolutely positive?'

Wendy replied, 'There were multiple witnesses. Some bloke in overalls with a bright red American baseball cap came out of the bush just prior to the smoke and fire starting. One firey happened to see him so he went to investigate. Stopped the flames from spreading but he discovered all the hallmarks of arson . . . accelerant, timed devices . . . This crim knows exactly what he's doing, all right. Drove away in an old green and brown army Jeep. Camouflage, I reckon.'

That was terrible! Aussies were used to the perils of bushfires raging through our Sclerophyll forests, sometimes ravaging homes, native fauna and occasionally even taking people's lives. But an arsonist was the worst sort of criminal.

Wendy had more to add. 'Chris and the rest of the force have been trying to catch him, checking vehicle records but he's slippery as a platypus. He's using false number plates.'

I hugged my landlady. Her brother and hubby were both putting their lives on the line to protect us from this man.

'There's one more thing, Debra. All of the fires, they've been both sides of the Derwent River, up near Mount Wellington and New Norfolk, yet none near the Glen Huon and Huon valleys. Nothing.'

I understood her reasoning. There had been a ring of fire around us.

'He lives here, doesn't he?' I stated. Arsonists lighting fires in their own backyards weren't very sensible. Travelling would deflect attention from their base of operations. 'Let's hope they catch him soon, Wendy. Robbie mentioned there's a heatwave forecast with high winds. If he lights his fires then . . .'

'Hell on earth, Debra.'

136

We were both subdued for a while, lost in our own private thoughts. Finally, Wendy suggested a mosey around the property. We grabbed our Akubra hats and sunnies and went outside.

The sun was warm though not oppressive. To the south, the steep slope that was dotted with blackwoods and gums had appeared serene and majestic earlier. Now, all I could imagine was a hillside where flames would race downward, ash and embers being blown as a vanguard to ignite vegetation below. This beautiful property would be engulfed in scant minutes.

Wendy's cattle dog ran up to us, eager to please her mistress before disappearing to chase the odd rabbit or brightly garbed rosella.

'You have cattle.' I could see them grazing.

'Beef cattle. You'll be well-fed with quality steaks here, Debra. Much better than that Woolies rubbish. Lot less work than dairy cows. There's my off-sider over there, fixing a fence.'

Wendy called out and the lithe youth waved back from across the sunburned field.

'Hans is from the Netherlands. Word of warning though. Don't call it Holland. You'll end up never hearing the end of it. Lovely boy apart from his country-name obsession. He's only here a couple of days a week but he wants full-time. Can't afford it though, even if he is a great worker. Easy on the eye too, if you understand my drift.'

'Not for me, Wendy. Shane's put me right off blokes, at least for a while.'

Wendy put an arm on my shoulder. 'They're not all bad, Debra. Chris came along when I was feeling much as you are now. My childhood wasn't the best and I had a lot of self-worth issues. Chris helped restore the girl I once was before . . . well, let's say my father was a verbal bully, putting us down all the time. Mum too.'

'Sorry to hear that. Robbie mentioned you'd been burned as well, and that's why he became a firefighter.'

She stopped. 'Robbie told you that? I suppose he would.' It was a mysterious comment to make.

I went on to explain that I'd had my own issues with losing my mother at a young age but Dad had helped me through. At least I thought he had. In retrospect, choosing Shane might indicate I'd been searching for a part of my life I'd missed and it was only now I understood that Shane had been a user, preying on that vulnerability.

I took a moment to listen to the country sounds. Sheep from a neighbour's farm, the cattle we were going to see and the myriad birds cheeping and squawking as they flew overhead.

'Wendy. I'm guessing there's more to cattle farming than sticking them in a field and telling them 'Go, girls. I'll see you in a few months.''

Wendy laughed out loud. 'Typical flaming townie! Even my small herd keeps me on my toes with vaccinations, worming, feeding and vet's bills. We have a few sheep as well, down by the creek.' She indicated a tall copse of gums down towards the Huon.

By the time we returned to the house, both of us were thirsty. Heather was waiting, dressed in jeans. Like all sensible country people her jeans were tucked into her thick socks. There were some nasty reptiles and insects out there, especially jack-jumper ants — enormous, black and mean as any creature I'd ever met. She brought us some chilled drinks, telling her mum she'd tended to the cat, dog and the chooks. I was surprised she didn't have a pony but Wendy explained none of them had bothered with riding and besides, Heather had other interests, sketching being her latest passion.

As I sipped my cola, I leaned back, examining the gallery. It was canary yellow with photos and paintings dotted around the walls. Here and there were excellent sketches of animals — Heather's, I assumed. The large waving branches shaded the row of windows from too much sunlight.

'Spaghetti tonight. Chris loves Italian

food. Hope you do too,' Wendy said to me.

'You bet.' Then I wondered, 'It's not out of a tin, is it?' That had been Shane's idea of an exotic meal. What had I seen in him?

'Alphabet spaghetti? My, that brings back memories!' Her happy expression clouded over for a moment. I could only guess at life with her father. 'No. It's a proper recipe from that Graham Kerr chef. A friend of mine recommended it.'

I stood to examine two strange circles neatly sketched on card and framed separately. Each was divided into twelve sectors with strange symbols neatly done with calligraphy arranged randomly. A key with those symbols and numbers was underneath.

'May I ask what these are, Wendy?'

'Birth charts, sometimes called natal charts. How the stars and planets were aligned when Chris and I were born. Mine's on the left. Heather's is in her room. I drew them up years ago.'

Robbie had mentioned Wendy's hobby

before I'd met her and I was curious.

'Astrology? I never pegged you for that. You're a trained science teacher. I would have thought the two were mutually exclusive. Do you believe that our lives are influenced by astral movements, depending on when we're born?'

'Oh, there's some absolute rubbish like the daily horoscope in the paper. Interestingly the Hobart paper is called the Mercury which, if you recall from astronomy at school is a planet. And in astrology Mercury symbolised communication. This is its symbol, here.' She indicated a circle with a plus sign underneath and horns on top. 'You've heard of Copernicus, haven't you?'

My science was rusty but not that rusty.

'The astronomer who suggested the sun was the centre of the Solar System, and not the Earth. Since the church always maintained the Earth was the centre of the universe, he wasn't too popular with them, if I recall.'

'Actually, the Catholic church did

accept his theory but the Reformation denounced his ideas as heresy. The point was, he believed in astrology.'

From a dresser drawer, Wendy extracted an Ephemeris with tables showing positions of planets in the sky with angles for each day in the past fifty years up to 1965.

'Astrology is an exact science in so many ways. What's your date of birth?' I told her, watching as she made a note of it. 'Time?'

'Six-fifteen at night, I believe. Don't remember, myself,' I grinned.

'And place?'

'Launceston? Are the stars that particular?'

'Six o'clock at night in Tassie would be eight in the morning GMT in London. The moon would be rising there as it's setting here. It's a small difference. Listen. Could I do an astrological chart for you? Perhaps then you'd have an inkling about my hobby.'

It was at that moment I recalled a comment I made to Robbie. 'I'm an

Aries, the ram. That's a fire sign, right?'
I checked out the charts on display.
'And you're a Leo. What's Robbie?'

Wendy hesitated, possibly suspecting
where this was going. 'He's a Scorpio, a
water sign. He's sensitive, craves secu-
rity and is intuitive. Did you realise he
has a yacht? Loves to go sailing.'

'As a matter of interest, are fire and
water signs compatible?'

Wendy fidgeted. 'Well, not really.
Scorpios are deep thinkers and logical,
whereas Arians are prone to emotional
outbursts. Fire and water don't mix
without a lot of steam! Why? Don't tell
me you fancy him?'

I scoffed. 'He's a friend, that's all.'

'You could do a lot worse. I love my
little brother, though he has issues from
his younger days, but he's a caring and
gentle man.'

'I'm surprised he's not married by now.'

Wendy avoided my gaze, staring out
the window to the concrete path that
led to the door.

'He never had a proper girlfriend, if

you must know, though he'd probably say otherwise to keep his ego intact. He has his reasons but it's not my place to elaborate. However, he's a dedicated volunteer in a very dangerous profession. Robbie hates fire with a vengeance.'

'He told me that his mate, Jimmy, had been a Fire Chief before him. And that he was one of the men who'd brought him back from his 'bad boy' days. Was Chris the other one?'

'Yes, my darling Chris. He and Robbie are such great buddies these days, though ten years ago it was a totally different story.'

That explained a great deal. Robbie's motivation was to help the community and repent for whatever past indiscretions he'd made. What had Wendy said — that he hated fires? Because they were wild and destructive and unpredictable, presumably. His words in the school parking lot came to mind.

'Wendy? When Robbie saw me getting frustrated with my car, I kinda lost my temper. After that, he referred to me as a human firestorm. That wasn't a compliment, was it?'

My eyes began to mist over as I struggled to retain whatever composure I could.

'It was just an expression, Debra. One said without thinking. We all do that.'

'Perhaps . . .'

I prayed she was right. Though I'd met him only a few days before, the last thing I wanted was for Robbie to despise me. I was better than my behaviour in that car park. No excuses that it was all Shane's fault. He wasn't even there, and we were well and truly finished. From this point on, it was up to me, and me alone, to control my volatile feelings.

★ ★ ★

Saturday came and brought a dull, overcast sky with it. I'd decided to spend the day in Hobart, collecting the last of my meagre possessions from Carrie-Anne's, say my goodbyes and my thanks for letting me crash at her place. Then I'd head down to the newly opened Wrest Point Casino to discover what the fuss was all about.

I'd booked a buffet lunch for two. Yes, two.

Robbie had surprised me during school on Friday, by offering to assist with the heavy boxes and records at Carrie-Anne's. It hadn't been totally altruistic on his part. He'd told me that there were materials for the alarm system which he'd ordered from a wholesaler in Hobart.

'There's little point in us going there in separate cars, Debra. Besides, that tiny Dinky toy of yours is hardly big enough to carry much. My station wagon makes more sense.'

It would, I'd thought — provided he emptied out the accumulated mound of crisp packets and boxes scattered throughout the interior!

'Sounds good, though I was planning having lunch at Wrest Point. It's time I checked it out. Would you like to join me?'

His reply was clipped. 'I don't approve of gambling, as you well know.'

I'd put my hand on his. He'd been in my classroom, attaching wiring to the once useless alarm. There hadn't been anyone else there to notice what could have been regarded as an intimate moment. Interestingly he hadn't flinched though the pulse rate that my fingers sensed in his wrist had increased.

'I understand. My reasons for going are for the food. Apparently, the inexpensive buffet has loads of local seafood like abalone, lobster and salmon. Don't you fancy some of that?'

His tensed muscles had relaxed a little. 'Abalone, eh? And you did say cheap?'

'It's an all-you-can-eat. There's a hotel there too. The gambling is just one aspect of the place. I don't gamble either.'

'Not even sweepstakes for the Melbourne Cup?' Robbie was testing me.

I responded with, 'Scout's honour. Well, Girl Guides, actually. I'm not a gambler, Robbie, but that doesn't stop me wanting to find out what Wrest

148

Point is like and enjoying a meal there. You coming with me then?'

'You've twisted my arm, Miss Winters. I'll come. And in return I'd like to take you sailing on Sunday — unless you have other plans?'

'None. Sailing sounds great.'

★ ★ ★

Robbie surprised me when he came to collect me. Not only was his wagon cleaned inside and out, so was Robbie. He'd scrubbed up pretty well, sporting a clean, crisp shirt and tie, slacks and almost matching socks. He'd overdone it with the Old Spice though. When would men learn less is more? Then it hit me. Robbie had no sense of smell so he'd splashed it on purely for my benefit.

I had chosen a fetching red and orange frock. After all, Wrest Point was to be Tassie's equivalent of the Monte Carlo casino straight out of the James Bond movies. I doubted we'd be

149

permitted to enter wearing thongs on our feet or turning up in a grubby T-shirt.

Firstly, he called to his supplier to collect the small but crucial electrical gizmos, then we headed off to Carrie-Anne's.

To be honest, his masculine strength was required for some of my boxes of books, especially negotiating the stairs. Despite not appearing to be much in my room, my remaining possessions did fill the back of the station wagon. As he made his way down the stairs with the final load of boxes, I said my goodbyes to Carrie-Anne.

'Just friends, eh?' she teased. 'Tell you what, my little best buddy, you could have fooled me. Did you notice the way he kept looking at you? I'd say he fancies you, Miss Debra Winters. And with those muscles and gorgeous eyes, I can see you two going places — and I bags bridesmaid!'

I pooh-poohed her suggestions.

'I told you, babe. I don't want a

relationship just now. I can't turn my affection switch on and off, like you. What is it now? Mr Wonderful number thirteen?' It was a standing joke between us. Carrie-Anne enjoyed playing the field, embracing the Sixties revolution with both hands!

It was off to Wrest Point after that, a short drive south of Hobart alongside the Derwent River. By now the sun had reappeared, glistening off the tranquil waters as we approached our destination. The parking lot was half full with vehicles, many Mercedes, Alfas and other high-end rentals, in addition to some expensive sports cars.

In the air-conditioned foyer, a man in a dark suit and waistcoat approached us. 'May I assist you, madam, sir?' He was quite polite.

I giggled, whispering to Robbie, 'I thought madams ran brothels,' before regaining my composure to request directions to the buffet.

I felt a little out of my comfort zone. The British had a word for it — 'posh'

— from the days when the landed gentry requested Port Outward Starboard Home on their ship journeys to India so as to avoid being too hot in their cabins in the sub-equatorial sun. It was a good word, but one that wasn't used by most Aussies.

I hoped the hardly-ever-used mascara wasn't over the top, my clutch bag matching my stilettos.

'You look spectacular, Debra. Apologies — should have told you that earlier. The red dress against your tan. You're really . . . '

'Hot? Like a firestorm?' I interjected.

'No. I was going to say like a gorgeous movie star. That 'firestorm' comment I made . . . it might have come out wrong, though it was a compliment, despite what you and Wendy think.'

If it was an apology, it was a good one. And he wasn't finished.

'I've never met anyone like you before. You're beautiful, smart and you speak your mind. That's what I love about you — ' He blushed.

'Did you just say the 'L' word?' I was somewhat taken aback!

Robbie was flustered. So, I did the only thing I could to make this awkward situation vanish. I gave him a kiss. It wasn't a tip-toey kiss on the lips, just a friendly peck on the cheek. Judging from his passive acceptance, it succeeded.

'Let's eat, Debra. Just don't make a piggy of yourself with all these delicacies up for grabs.'

It was a joke and I accepted it as such, though the 'piggy' reference wasn't all that endearing.

Being greedy would have been so easy with mouth-watering salads, a carvery displaying duck, lamb, venison and other meats. There was everything a discerning diner could ever want.

We promenaded around the refrigerated tables. Fifteen different desserts beckoned, and we weren't the only diners who stood there amazed. It was a leisurely meal in lovely ambient surroundings. When we did eventually leave, we were both sated, with me feeling that I wouldn't need to eat for a week.

Robbie accepted that the meal was subsidised to draw guests into visiting, then indulging in a flutter or two on the blackjack tables. The revolving restaurant was only accessible to diners and in true Tassie fashion it took its time at one revolution every ninety minutes, fast enough to appreciate the views on the mountain, river and Hobart skyline without making you motion-sick.

Watching some women decked out in jewels and sequined gowns at lunch was a bit much for Tassie but if it made them feel 'posh', I supposed there was no harm in it. Fur stoles in summer were a bit pretentious, though. When I pointed out one wannabe film star, Robbie commented about mutton dressed as lamb just a touch too loudly. Most gave a sly smile, though the lady in question gave him a dirty look before flinging her dead animal over her shoulder and storming off.

I shushed him too late to which he

replied, 'You're the brightest star in here, Debra, and I don't care who hears me.'

What was going on? Robbie was being too inconsistent for my mind to deal with. Did he fancy me, or not? Every time I tried to get close, he drew back. If he was afraid of something, I doubted it was me. All I could think of was the childhood trauma Wendy alluded to. He was in his late twenties yet wasn't married and apparently hadn't had a serious relationship. If anyone were a walking contradiction, it was my Robbie.

My Robbie? What on earth was going through my head? He wasn't mine! I was still raw from Shane's betrayal, consciously trying not to over-compensate with another man on the rebound.

Yet everything I saw in Robbie highlighted the fact that life with Shane had been so shallow, and that we'd had little in common apart from teaching English. Robbie was so different. We'd connected instantly as friends and, right now, that's all I wanted. Saying that, it felt strangely as if we were a couple and I had to remind myself that we weren't. Part of me wanted to take his hand in mine. I fought that temptation.

'Can I ask a stupid question, Robbie?' I asked as we made our way through the complex, marvelling at the ornate decor and furnishings.

'Ask away, Miss Winters.'

'Do you like the Dave Clark Five?'

Did he even know who they were? Shane didn't.

'Sure. Love their stuff. Why?'

I smiled, then took his hand in mine. 'No reason. Just getting to know my new best friend.'

By this time, we'd reached the casino rooms. One-armed bandits or poker machines were arranged row upon row. Over half had someone seated in front of them, feeding them change like a mother feeding an insatiable infant. It was a major surprise. These weren't the idle rich who could afford to lose money on a whim. Their clothing and appearance told me they were ordinary

156

hard-working Tasmanians.

Two rows over, her face almost hidden behind a machine, there was a woman I recognised. We approached her, Robbie still holding my hand.

'Mrs Pilkington? It's me, Debra Winters.'

The cleaner from my old school looked up momentarily. She had a dazed, almost trance-like look on her wrinkled face. 'Oh, it's you, Debra. Isn't this place wonderful? I can come here every day to be with my friends.'

Her friends were presumably the other zombies scattered around the room, all mechanically pulling the lever of their machines, hoping the next roll of the tumblers would be the one.

I moved away quickly, hurrying out of the oppressive room to the decking outside, overlooking the waters.

'What's the matter, Debra?' Robbie inquired gently, pulling me to his chest as I began to sob.

'That . . . that lovely woman. I've known her for years. She doesn't have any money

157

to spare. This place might help restore Tassie's economy, but at what cost?'

I stood back to dry my eyes with my hanky. This was becoming a habit, crying like an emotional schoolgirl, yet Robbie wasn't judging me.

Or was he? His grin suggested there was something wrong with me.

'Panda eyes?' Damn. My mascara had run.

'Just like Dusty,' he told me.

Great. Being a Dusty Springfield look-alike was not on my agenda for today. I excused myself to repair the damage.

Robbie then suggested we head for the coffee lounge. Our buffet lunch included after-meal drinks there. Once we sat down, it was time to apologise for my previous neutral stance on gambling.

'I know that lady we met struggles to make ends meet. Seeing her spending what little she has on some impossible dream opened my eyes.'

Australia had always been a nation of chancers, ready to put their last dollar on some nag at the racecourse who was a 'dead cert' to win. The entire country almost ground to a standstill the first Tuesday afternoon in November for the Melbourne Cup. We Tasmanians had our own horse-racing and now our own high-end casino.

I explained my change of heart to Robbie. Not everyone was as strong-willed as me when it came to resisting the prospect of 'This time I'll win'. People like Mrs Pilkington might have a fleeting buzz of a dream prize, but the disappointment that came later must have been crushing. And yet they came back. Was it an addiction?

Or was I being too judgmental?

Robbie chose to elaborate on his concerns.

'You recall I mentioned Jimmy Jordan. He was my mentor when I was a bit of a toe-rag years ago. It was the second time he'd come to my rescue. Anyway, Jimmy suggested I join up as a volunteer firey. He knew my feelings about fire out of control. A . . . a mate of mine got badly burned once. Stuffed his life up good and proper.'

First his sister being burned, then a mate? No wonder he felt the way he did. Firefighting was a dangerous job that most people would shy away from. Sure, there was that glamour that attracted young boys to pretend with their Matchbox or Corgi fire trucks, yet when they grew up and understood the perils, most chose more sedate jobs. Thank goodness there were some who took on the role.

'Jimmy taught me a lot about life. So did Chris in a different way. It was Jimmy who taught me self-discipline, to funnel the anger deep inside into something positive.'

He paused, gazing through the tinted panoramic glass toward the riverside. A family were seated by the bank, two kiddies frolicking on the narrow river beach with a ball and buckets of sand.

'Trouble is, Jimmy's getting on a bit, started drinking too much at the pub every day.' He sipped his lukewarm coffee. 'Gambling as well. Never had any kids — apart from me, I guess. He was the father figure I never had. His wife, Yvonne, eventually left after far too many ultimatums and that didn't help. These days, I'm all he has left of his old life. He hardly works any more.'

Jimmy had saved Robbie and he wanted to stand by his old mate. I suspected it was a losing battle but Robbie continued to try.

'You took over as Fire Chief when Jimmy couldn't hack it?' I suggested, softly. 'I'd like to meet him some day.'

'And why's that, Debra?'

'Because he's important in your life. He's your mate. I reckon that's reason enough, don't you?'

'Sorry, of course it is. It's just I've been doing this alone for so long. Chris and Wendy washed their hands of Jimmy ages ago. He's not an easy bloke to deal with nowadays. Mood swings, swearing. He's got a twin brother in Sydney but he hasn't seen him in years. They were never close. Told me on a visit about five years ago.'

161

★ ★ ★

Returning to The Valley was like leaving reality and dropping down some Lewis Carroll rabbit hole. There was a barrier between Hobart and the Huon, the steep slopes of Mount Wellington a natural barrier between two differing worlds.

The left-hand side had only a metal rail to protect us from a long fall for much of the early journey. Luckily, there was nothing else in sight. Then an old car pulled out from a side gravel road, moving slightly slower than us.

I noticed a metal box under the middle of Robbie's dashboard. An attached microphone was hooked on the side just by my knee.

'What's this?' I asked him.

'Two-way radio. Essential if I'm on call. We firemen have our own frequency, amateur radio hams have another.'

'And radio stations are on others still.' I understood a bit about communications. 'Having your own two-way

162

radio sounds very exciting.'

'Not as exciting as dealing with fires. Actually 'exciting' isn't the right term. 'Scary as blazes,' more like. You have to trust your teammates implicitly. As for the guy lighting those latest fires . . . ' He clenched his hands.

'Calm down. Hey — that car up ahead. Looks more like a Jeep. You don't suppose . . . ?'

We moved closer. The driver wore a red hat. The arsonist the police were searching for? Robbie realised it too.

'Debra. You need to call this in on the radio. Flip the power switch on the front. I'll tell you how to use it.' But before I could, the Jeep sped up. So did we — and we were faster.

Grasping that same fact, the Jeep driver braked then turned precariously onto another dirt road, spitting a cloud of dust and pebbles into the air.

'Hold on!' shouted Robbie as he too swerved. The powerful car began to tip on its side as the wheels on my side left the ground.

'Robbie!' I shrieked, grabbing vainly at the dash. A giant tree loomed in front of us at an impossible angle, my body straining against the seat belt. We were going over . . .

164

8

The car crashed back down to the ground, grinding to a halt scant metres from the scribbly gum tree.

'You OK, Debra?'

'Yes. I think so. You?'

'That piercing scream of yours didn't do my ears any good, but yeah, I'm in one piece. Looks like Mr Red Cap got away, though.'

We both stepped out. Robbie checked the tyres and suspension. I examined my possessions which fortunately didn't include breakables. The Holden was a solid workhorse and in one piece.

Although I told Robbie I was all right, I had bruises in places a young lady didn't like to mention. I only hoped they wouldn't spoil our day out on Sunday sailing on the Good Ship Lollipop.

★ ★ ★

That night, after tea, I sat quietly while Chris, Wendy and Heather talked between themselves. There was an Alistair MacLean novel open in my hands but I couldn't concentrate on it. Nevertheless, it was an excuse not to join in.

I wanted some quiet time to reflect on the past week. It was the mysterious Robbie I was focused on, though I chose not to make that public knowledge. Robbie had secrets, and secrets between a man and a woman were never good.

'You OK, Debra?' Wendy called out, echoing her brother's question from after the car chase.

'Yeah, just reading.' I held up the open book.

'You do realise it's a lot easier to understand when it's the right way up,' Wendy commented, causing a laugh all around, especially from me.

Busted. I put the offending novel on the table by my side. 'I was wondering if I might use the kitchen? I fancied doing pies for tomorrow.'

'You do realise that glorified row boat of his is literally called Titanic Two, don't you?' Chris interjected with a chuckle.

'Of course you can use the kitchen. In fact, mind if I join you? There's nothing on telly apart from cop shows.'

I was pleasantly surprised. Normally I'd found women to be quite protective of their kitchen space. My suspicion was she'd chosen this as an excuse for a woman to woman catch-up.

My plan was to make cheese and onion pies to take on Robbie's boat, or ship, or whatever it was called. I was not a water person. Certainly, it was fine to watch waves from afar and I wasn't a great swimmer. I floundered rather than breaking records in breast-stroke races in school. On the other hand, I did win the prize for best dog-paddle when I was fourteen.

I'd never been on a boat in my life. If Chris had been honest about the Titanic Two, that didn't help allay my apprehensions. The only consolation was the chance of encountering any icebergs on the Huon in this weather were slim. Even so . . .

However, Wendy was wonderful to speak to. Being a teacher too, we had much to discuss while she helped me prepare the two pies for cooking. We ended up doing more Sunday lunch as well.

Wendy explained how frustrated she was by the actions — or lack thereof — of All Saints' science teacher. Despite a lab full of equipment and chemicals, Martin Day's lessons consisted of reading from text books. No experiments, like burning magnesium, making fruity smelling esters, dissecting rats. Nothing. He didn't even do demonstrations from the front desk.

I'd never realised. What was science without a Bunsen burner or zapping your best friend with static electricity? Any enthusiasm for the subject would evaporate.

There was little Wendy could do

about it — or me — since Mr Day was a part of the furniture at All Saints, and that furniture was decayed, mouldy and ancient. Yet Martin was clinging on, refusing to move aside or update his archaic mode of teaching. Wendy was right. My school was replete with dinosaurs, relics of bygone times. Could Doris, Ken and I hope to change the status quo?

As we talked, it was apparent that I was avoiding any mention of Robbie. If Wendy noticed, she kept her own counsel.

That night in bed, I was still puzzled about Robbie's secret past and wondered if I might find out the truth. Part of me hoped I would — though another part was a little afraid of those hidden aspects of Robbie Sanderson.

★ ★ ★

Chris wasn't kidding about the name of Robbie's tiny yacht. The resplendent blue and white livery of the paintwork

169

shone against the azure waters near the mooring at Port Huon. The Huon was about a kilometre wide at this point, even though we'd had so little rain.

'For heaven's sake, Debra. You only need one flotation vest.'

'You can never be too careful,' I reminded him.

Gingerly stepping onto a tiny boat, we rowed over to his yacht. It was not my idea of spacious with only a shoebox-sized cabin under the mast.

'Are you certain you know what you're doing?'

'Dead cert. You'll need this, me hearty.' He passed me a black eye patch along with a black cap with a white Jolly Roger emblazoned on it.

'You're a right galah, you! You must have an entire mob of kangaroos loose in that top paddock of yours,' I said, playfully tapping his head.

As time ticked by, it became apparent that Robbie was a skilled yachtsman. Slowly, I relaxed my white-knuckled grip on the side, beginning to enjoy the

170

experience. The wind whipped through my hair as the sounds and smells of the mighty river assaulted me with their enticing power. We tacked through the waves, moving upstream towards the riverside township of Franklin.

For lunch, we anchored in a mirror-smooth bay. Robbie suggested I could go for a swim if I wanted to. The weather was definitely warm enough for it. I'd made certain my easily sun-burned skin was liberally plastered with sunblock as well as covering my very prominent nose with white zinc cream.

'No cossie,' I apologised. 'And there's no possibility of me going skinny-dipping, even though I'm sure you'll suggest it. Why don't you dive in? I'd love to see that muscular torso of yours uncovered.'

A shadow clouded his features. 'I'll keep my T-shirt on, thanks, but yeah, a dip does sound tempting, Miss Winters. You could be my one-woman cheering squad.'

Immediately he dived in, presumably

confident that the water was deep enough. Vigorous freestyle strokes took him metres away so rapidly, I wondered if my Robbie were part fish. I clapped enthusiastically as he demonstrated his prowess, switching seamlessly between breaststroke, free-stroke and even the very exhausting butterfly.

When he clambered back on board, I suggested again that he take off his T-shirt. The outline of his taut stomach and muscular chest showed through the dripping wet material.

'Not today. Messy sunburn you wouldn't want to see. If you're that desperate I'll let you touch my biceps.' There he was, flirting again.

'No thanks. Might put me off my picnic lunch,' I joked back, opening the basket I'd brought.

★ ★ ★

The day's sailing was over too quickly. Returning to shore, we bade farewell to the 'good ship Titanic Two' then set off back to my lodgings.

'Would it be OK to take a detour via Jimmy's? It'd be a chance for you to meet. I may have mentioned you once or twice when I last visited.'

I was in no rush. 'Sounds good, Robbie.'

Jimmy's place was deep in the bush with an overgrown gravel track the sole access. Although it was a typical weatherboard structure, a new-ish galvanized shed was the most striking feature.

I wasn't prepared for the sight that greeted me. It was a disappointment to say the least. I doubted that any self-respecting spider would be seen within a mile of the place — or should I be saying one-point-six kilometres? It put me in mind of an Aussie version of the house in the *Psycho* movie. It had the same foreboding sense of gloom even though all around was bright sunshine.

Robbie appeared to be reading my mind. 'The place has gone downhill since Yvonne left.'

Downhill? The tumbledown shack had reached rock-bottom long ago. To spare Robbie's feelings, I said nothing.

'Have to warn you, Debra. It's tough on the nose in there. Jimmy's . . . well, he's let himself go as well as the house.'

I steeled myself. If Robbie thought it was whiffy with his lack of a sense of smell, heaven alone knew what delights I was going to experience.

Walking through the open door after knocking was something that would haunt me for some time.

Jimmy Jordan was seated on what was, in some former life, a lounge suite. At first, I smelled nothing — although it didn't take long for the stench to assail my senses. I fought to keep from gagging, trusting that my nose would eventually get used to it. It didn't.

My shoes trod on something sticky. The overflowing ashtray had butts and ash on the less than pristine table and floor with half-emptied bottles of beer littering most of the room. Jimmy, or at least the man I presumed was Robbie's mate, opened one lazy eye and closed it again. He was sprawled across the seat, his chest barely covered by a stained shirt.

'Whatcha want, Robbie?' he drawled before wiping his arm over his lips. As he spoke I saw that at least one tooth was missing. The horse racing was on the old TV, the sound turned down.

'Wanted to check in, see how you are, mate.'

This time both his eyes opened. He saw me, then lazily scratched his upper leg, maybe to embarrass me.

'Notice you brung her even when I told you didn't want no stuck-up sheila comin' round.'

I bristled at the insult. Jimmy was not someone I'd normally stay in the same room with — yet he was a friend of Robbie's. Though for the life of me, I couldn't see why.

There was a plaque on the stone chimney breast. In a room of dirt and garbage, it shone as though recently polished. Another odour touched my senses. Some sort of medication? I couldn't place it.

'Nice to meet you, Mr Jordan. I'm Deb — '

'Don't care who you are, girlie. You're not welcome in this . . . ' he waved one arm. 'This here grand establishment.' He sniggered before bursting into a coughing fit. It was obvious there was no point trying to be friendly with him so I stepped away, moving to examine the plaque. It was in recognition of his services to the Tasmanian Fire Services.

It was while standing there that I noticed another smell — like some dead animal, probably under the dirt-stained floorboards.

'Oi, you! Get away from there!' Jimmy shouted, getting rapidly to his feet. He made a move to grab my arm but Robbie intervened, stepping to block his advance. My friend glanced back at me, turning his back on Jimmy.

'You OK, Deb — ' he began before I gasped, pointing at Jimmy behind him.

Robbie turned back immediately, shielding me with his body.

'Jimmy had a rifle in his hands. Where had he grabbed that from? Before either of us could react, the weapon was pointed at us.

'Jimmy. What are you do — '

'Told you not to bring no one else here, Robbie. Now you'll have to pay.'

Then he fired the rifle.

9

Dust and chucks of ceiling plaster showered down upon us, covering us in debris. We were both cowering and shocked by the ferocity of Jimmy's anger.

'Get out!' Jimmy levelled the rifle at me.

'We're going, Jimmy.' Robbie made certain he stayed between me and the madman as we fled, driving away as quickly as we could.

A mile or so down the track, Robbie stopped his vehicle, his hands shaking uncontrollably.

'I'm ... I'm so ve-very s-sorry, Debra,' he stammered. 'Should never ... never have taken you there. I've never seen him like that before.'

I was still in shock myself. My knees were drawn up to my chest as I tried to curl into a ball.

'What just happened? That rifle?'

'I didn't realise he had one. Just . . . just give me a moment.'

Robbie stepped outside, dusted himself off then placed his hands on the roof. The sobbing was quiet for a moment, before erupting into a howl of frustration.

I stayed inside. There were my own demons to deal with. I could have been killed.

A minute passed, maybe two. Robbie opened his door and popped his head in.

'You all right?'

Slowly I put my feet back in the footwell.

'Sort of,' I mumbled. Then I turned to face him. 'Robbie, you have to . . .'

'I know.' He reached over to unhook the microphone from the two-way radio set under the dashboard before straightening up to stand outside the car. His other hand was clenching and unclenching constantly.

'Robbie to base, Robbie to base. Over.'

The speaker near me erupted with static before a female voice answered.

'Base here, Chief. How can I help? Over.'

'Can you patch me through to the police, please, Rhonda? Jimmy just threatened us with a rifle. Over.'

There was a pause. 'Jimmy? A rifle? No! Sorry, Robbie. Patching you through now, Chief.'

I half-heard Robbie describing what had occurred. Even a shot being fired over someone's head was a major incident here in Tassie. I imagined armed police being dispatched.

Jimmy Jordan had scared me more than anyone in my whole life, yet I doubted he'd ever have really injured me. Was he drunk? Did he resent me for 'stealing' his friend? If Robbie hadn't stepped in front of me, would he . . . ?

I shuddered, my blood running cold.

What if Jimmy came after us? I twisted my head to peer through the rear window for any sign he was coming.

Robbie signed off with an 'Over and

180

out'. He sat back into the car and took a deep breath.

'They're on their way, Debra . . . the cops.'

I checked the road behind once more in the vanity mirror on the sun-visor.

'Robbie? Can we go now, please?'

'Yeah, sure.' He turned the ignition on and was about to shift the column selector on the steering wheel to D for Drive when he faced me.

'I'm so sorry I put you in danger, Debra.'

I put my hand reassuringly on his. 'I don't blame you, Robbie. But Jimmy . . . he's out of control.'

'Yeah. I realise that now.'

I nodded, keeping my hand on his knee as we drove, to reassure him I was fine.

Arriving back at the Powell's, Wendy and Chris came out to greet us. Presumably the local police station had filled Chris in. Wendy comforted me while Robbie went off with Chris. I guessed it was to give him the whole story and make a statement. I'd have to do that as well, I supposed.

Saying goodbye to Robbie later that evening was awkward. In the end I gave him a peck on the cheek and a sort of hug. I thought that was the end of the drama and that my life would return to normal after that. How wrong could I be?

★ ★ ★

Chris told us that evening that three armed officers had been dispatched to Jimmy's home. They'd found no one in spite of a detailed search. His old EJ Holden was gone. The general consensus was that he'd gone bush.

He knew the forests better than most and could have been anywhere. Chris decided to leave it a day or two then send his men out there again. Meanwhile, officers were advised to keep a watch for him. He was described as armed and potentially dangerous.

Being on call this week, Robbie's

time at the school would be restricted. His priority was to protect the community from fires, if the need arose.

★ ★ ★

On Monday, Ken asked me to wait after school so he could discuss a proposal with me. From the tone of his voice, I'd at last be getting answers to that puzzling conversation we'd had soon after I'd begun teaching there. Not that I was concerned about whatever he'd have to say. I wished I hadn't drunk quite as much as I had last night, but Wendy had insisted the alcohol would help relax me after the near-death experience.

It had helped, even though right now I wondered if this day-after beer-induced headache was worse than dwelling on the memory of that rifle.

The kids had helped keep my mind off revisiting those anxious moments. Chris had made Ken aware of what I'd been through and he'd been as supportive as he could. No one else in the school had been told, and that suited me.

A few times when a door banged shut in the breeze, I jumped, causing a few giggles in the class. I could deal with that. If they thought I was a 'fraidy-cat' then so be it. Events like yesterday made the trauma of a bad-hair day pale into insignificance in the grand scheme of life.

The weather remained warm with calm summer breezes. However, the forecast for later in the month was a major concern to many adults, as well as my pupils. Memories of 1967 were still raw in the memories of all save the youngest.

During a free period, I chose to nip down to the local post office about two hundred yards from my classroom. There were some letters that needed posting to my dad.

I was beginning to recognise the friendly locals, many of whom knew me by name as a newcomer to the tight-knit community. In fact, one pretty dark-haired lady in her fifties went out of her way to be friendly. She was behind the counter. Although others were in the building, they were filling in forms on benches near the front window.

'You're the new schoolie, aren't you? I'm Agnes. Work here part-time. How are you finding the kids, then?'

'I'm Debra Winters. The kids are great, thanks, Agnes. I love the school. Friendly town, too.'

We continued talking with me telling her where I'd been brought up. Like many southerners, she'd never been to the north of Tassie and hadn't left our state at all. I could see why Tom wanted to travel and experience the wonders of the world. I'd managed a few months seeing parts of Britain and France, and hoped to return there in the future. My ancestors had emigrated from Wales to Tasmania over three generations ago, so there was a special family connection there.

★   ★   ★

It was four o'clock When Ken came to find me in my classroom. The bus loads of students had long since departed.

I hardly visited the staff room any longer after the initial daily briefing. The lingering cigarette smoke from my fellow teachers was too oppressive. It may have been anti-social of me in the eyes of some staff yet the dry air in combination with the acrid smoke did threaten to set off my slight asthma condition so I felt justified.

'Time for that special one-to-one, Debra. Might I suggest my office? It's more private than here. Also, I've bought a small fridge to store my . . . shall we say, 'brain food'?'

Brain food? Ahh . . . cold choccies!

'Lead on, Headmaster.' I grabbed my case and bulky handbag. What could he possibly wish to propose to me, I wondered? Nevertheless, I was very curious.

When we arrived, there was another

woman already there, sitting comfortably on one of the three armchairs. She was smartly dressed in slacks and a Paisley blouse, long platinum blonde hair cascading over her shoulders. I'd not seen here before. As Lewis Carroll's Alice would say, 'Curiouser and curiouser'.

A sheaf of papers was arranged on the round table in the middle. Ken checked the corridor outside before closing the door.

'Debra, this is Alison.'

We exchanged handshakes as she offered me some cake and a cold soft drink. The way she made herself at home in here was slightly disconcerting.

Ken loosened his tie, took a long sip of his beverage then rubbed his hands together before sitting forward to address me.

'I imagine you're wondering what this is all about. Alison here is your replacement,' he began.

The look of horror on my face must have spoken volumes because Alison immediately cuffed him on the arm.

'Ken, can't you see you're upsetting our guest. Honestly, some men!' She reached out to touch my shoulder. 'Apologies. Ken's quite excited over our proposition and isn't thinking straight. If he weren't such a loving hubby, I — '

'Husband?' I asked, none the wiser as to the reason I was here. 'You're not thinking of some ménage à trois, are you?' I joked.

Ken almost choked on his cake while Alison sat back, laughing. 'Hardly! You don't know my husband very well if you're worried about that.' She bent over to pretend-whisper in my ear. 'What we're proposing is far, far haughtier than that!'

She gave me a playful smile before sweeping a lock of errant hair from in front of her eye.

'You do realise Ken has a very high regard for you? You made an instant impression on that day for your job interview.'

'I'm flattered. Does that mean I'm

like a Teacher's Pet?'

I was dying to find out what was going on here, but this banter between the three of us was quite delicious, so I decided to wait for the big reveal.

I didn't have long to wait.

'Debra,' Ken teased, putting the cake down. 'I'd like you to be All Saint's Deputy Headmistress.'

This time, it was me who was flabbergasted. I was twenty-five years old, for goodness' sake! I'd only been teaching less than four years.

'But . . . but my age. I've never even been English Mistress.'

'Nonsense. You're English Mistress now.'

Alison was clearly adamant that I could have this new position if I wished. Between the two of them, I surmised, they'd already devised answers for every objection I might have to this idea.

'Technically,' I countered. 'I'm the only full-time English teacher. This is a case of one chief and absolutely no Indians.'

The whole conversation was surreal.

The very thought of me being promoted over all the other staff was making my head dizzy.

'We are serious, Debra. Ken suggested it to me the day he first interviewed you for your position here as a teacher. Haven't you wondered why there's no Deputy at All Saints?'

Taking a dainty bite from my second slice of cold devil's food cake, I had a fleeting thought that eating such food at a Catholic school might be inappropriate!

Then my brain kicked into the current discussion once more. The couple were awaiting my answer.

'Low enrolment numbers?' The school was barely viable with the number of pupils it had — or rather, the lack of them.

'No,' Ken explained. 'The simple fact was that no one was suitable — until you arrived. Let's examine the criteria . . . strong disciplinarian when required, check. Respected by staff and students alike, check. Effective with administrative tasks and dealing with Head Office, check. After all, you did sort out those petty idiots in Hobart. That was magic to behold! You are a natural for this role.'

He glanced across to Alison who nodded for him to continue.

'The main criteria, however,' is that you are passionate about the profession. You clearly want our school to be the best it can be. If anything, accepting my invitation will empower you to achieve those goals.'

Alison now joined in to remind me of those qualities which I never regarded as anything special about myself.

'Did you realise how highly respected you already are within this community? What you did about the Art Room fire is still the main topic of conversation whenever I'm in town. You have more friends here than you could imagine. There are another five new students coming next week. Even though they live locally, their parents had decided to bus them elsewhere because they had no faith in the future of the school.

With you here, they've had a change of heart.'

I relaxed back into my chair, only noticing I had a crumb on my lips when Alison touched her own.

'I have to say to both of you that it's a great deal to consider. This opportunity is such a shock. What if I can't live up to your expectations?'

'You'll have us to give you guidance, so it's not as though you'll be on your own.' Alison smiled at me warmly.

'There are benefits, too,' Ken added. 'More pay, of course — a lot more. Then there's less face-to-face teaching. And that's where Alison comes to the rescue. She's a qualified English teacher but, with our two young girls, she can only manage part-time. Your teaching load would reduce from twenty-eight periods a week to around fourteen. And of course, you get to choose which classes you keep on.'

'And my lunchtime remedial classes?'

'I would like for them to continue as normal. I've already seen a difference in the confidence of the students.'

That was encouraging to hear. I'd noticed that change, but if others had too, then something was going well.

'When do you require an answer, Ken?' It was a lot to think about.

'Shall we say in a week? I'll be sticking my neck out for you, Debra. There are a few teachers here who feel they're more entitled — as well as those pen-pushers in Hobart who'd run a mile if they had to stand in front of a bunch of kids. However, it's you I believe in, and I'm positive that together we could be a dream team! No more turning the staff room clock back, though . . .'

Ken gave me a cheeky grin.

I smiled too. 'I wondered if you noticed, Ken. I'm pleased to discover my little prank didn't escape your eagle eyes.'

The conversation continued for a while longer, each second making me realise the vast step we'd all be taking if I were to accept the offer. Still, I needed to discuss the pros and cons. Wendy was my first and only choice. I respected her opinion more than most people I'd ever met.

★ ★ ★

Returning home, I was bubbling with excitement.

Me — a Deputy Head? Could I handle it? Arranging cover for absent staff, as well as a myriad other tasks I could only guess at, would push me to my professional limit.

I was eager to share my news with Wendy — but she beat me to it.

'Something momentous is happening to you over the next week or so, Debra,' she proclaimed as I entered the gallery.

'It already has. How could you possibly have known?' Had Ken phoned her? No, that wasn't likely; they weren't friends or anything.

'It's in the stars, believe it or not. 'I've never seen anything like it.' She thrust two pages with detailed circles and scribbled notes in front of me. I

194

recognised them as a horoscope chart, split into the twelve houses with symbols everywhere and figures all over the page.

'Debra, this is your natal chart showing planetary aspects when you were born. The other chart is what's called a secondary progression chart drawn up for you now. See these planets, the sun and the moon all positioned this week and next week? The moon moves quickly compared to the others but do you see what's happening? That's an alignment, and —'

I couldn't wait any longer. 'Ken wants me to be Deputy Head!' I blurted out in my excitement.

Wendy stared at me blankly.

'Well you could at least pretend to be pleased,' I admonished, feeling slightly miffed.

'Sorry, Debra. Of course, that's fab news and you'll be brill in that job. It's just . . . well, what the stars are foretelling . . . it involves fire.'

I understood that she was simply

perplexed. After all that work drawing up the charts and she'd got it wrong.

'Maybe it was describing the Art Room fire and the stars had their dates mixed up,' was my suggestion.

'I don't think so, Debra. As for your promotion, there's a minor mention of it here in the Tenth House that represents your professional career. The Sixth House represents your daily work. Your natal chart has Sagittarius in the Tenth House, indicating you'll aspire to be a leader.'

'You're making that up after the event.'

'That's typical Aries scepticism, Debra. If you don't believe what I've already predicted, check out my notes on the table.'

I did. Promotion at work, extra responsibilities. It was all there, and more. Perhaps there was something to this astrology after all. The notes were untidy but the essence was there for me to read. *Fire!* was underlined a number of times.

I asked Wendy, 'Could all this fire stuff have a symbolic meaning, like passion or love?' I flushed and added quickly, 'Not that there's any of that around.'

'Like passion for your new role at school?'

I took a deep breath. That sounded like a reasonable answer.

'No, Debra. I'm no expert, you understand, but in this case, it is literal fire,' she insisted, stabbing at the pages with a finger. 'These planetary alignments are proclaiming that there's something dramatic afoot for you this week. And this good news about your promotion is only the tip of the iceberg.'

'Fire? Icebergs? Talk about mixed metaphors, Wendy! You've warned me, though — and as they say, forewarned is forearmed.'

Wendy poured water into the kettle, and took out two cups, spooning some chocolate powder into mine.

'OK, let's forget about metaphors and clichés, Debra. Now tell me everything that happened. I'm extremely happy for you.'

'First of all, I don't want you telling anyone else at the moment — and that includes Chris and Robbie. And definitely not Heather. I'm still considering the implications.'

Wendy agreed so I began, 'Well, Ken's wife, Alison, was there . . . '

★ ★ ★

It was over an hour later that Chris pulled up in a marked police cruiser.

To our surprise, Robbie was with him. They came in, both appearing anxious.

'When I arrived home,' Robbie explained, 'There was a note from Jimmy in the letterbox. He apologised profusely, blaming it on the drink. He wants you and me to come over at six-thirty. Said he'd hand himself in to the police at the same time. That's why Chris is here.'

I was perplexed.

'You want me to come? I don't know about that, Robbie. I'm sure he hates me for some reason.'

'I understand your reticence, Debra. I still think it would be good for you to meet the real Jimmy, though. There's a word . . . cath . . . cathar . . .'

'Catharsis. Releasing emotions from historical trauma. You may be right, although I'm worried.'

Robbie again offered reassurance for me to join him, saying, 'Chris will be there.'

I considered it momentarily. After all, Chris was armed and more than a match for the man who'd threatened me yesterday. And he had a radio to call for back-up.

'You can stay in the car until we're certain it's safe,' Robbie offered.

'OK,' I conceded, deciding to bid Wendy farewell before I had the time to change my mind.

'Remember to watch out for fire,' she warned.

Robbie must have overheard.

'No chance of that, big sis. Our arsonist friend seems to have gone quiet. Chasing him the other day must have made him realise things were getting too hot for him.'

I winced but Robbie seemed oblivious to the terrible pun he'd just made.

Facing Wendy, he went on, 'Are you talking about that silly horoscope rubbish again? You are, aren't you? And involving Debra, too? For a science teacher, you have some strange hobbies, Wendy.'

Chris and I smiled at the friendly bickering, not uttering a word. Perhaps he'd also seen her predictions come true.

★ ★ ★

The journey wasn't that far. The air-con was welcome though, even if I was seated in the back. Seat belt wearing was a relatively new law but I could appreciate the advantages — especially when Chris had to brake suddenly because of

200

animals dashing across the gravel track. Most of the time I stared out of the side window. The conversation between the guys up front was too difficult to make out so I simply zoned out.

The western sky filtered through the shiny gum leaves of the forest, but the blue was changing subtly to a pale grey. I must have been a little drowsy as I didn't realise the implications immediately. It was only when I sniffed the air that the reason became apparent.

'Smoke.'

The men sniffed too.

'I can't smell — ' Robbie began.

'Take no notice of him, Debra. I can smell it. There's a fire up ahead.'

'I can see flames. Over there,' I exclaimed, leaning forward and pointing between them to the right.

'That's Jimmy's place,' Robbie said, suddenly more alarmed.

By the time we turned into the large clearing surrounding the house, it was obvious that the building was a raging inferno, with great tongues of flame reaching a good eight metres.

Robbie was out before the car had even skidded to a halt. He vaulted over burning debris as he charged towards the holocaust, arm raised protectively before his face. The heat was stifling. Robbie stopped, then backed up, thinking with his head at last. To advance any closer would have been virtual suicide.

I was already scanning the surroundings . . . a hose was coiled up near the metal shed, and there was a large rainwater tank connected to the shed's downpipes.

'Hose, Robbie — over here!' I cried out, smoke blowing in my face. Without a pump the only pressure would be from gravity — however the tank was up high, taller than a man's height so there should be enough. We all ran over there, Robbie uncoiling the hose and snaking it towards the heart of the fire.

Meanwhile, I'd clambered up the wooden framework to yank the tap open. My dress blew around in the wind but this was no time to worry about modesty.

Then I tapped the side of the corrugated tank to determine how full it was. The dull thud became more of an echo about four feet from the bottom.

'Sounds half full, Robbie,' I shouted, my hands cupped around my mouth. The sound of crackling wood from the ravenous fire was hard to be heard over so I tried again, waving one arm furiously. This time he acknowledged me, waving back.

Over at the police car, Chris was standing outside, speaking on the radio. Reinforcements would be soon on their way.

Although sparks and embers were falling on the bare earth of the home surrounds, it was the threat of the surrounding shrivelled vegetation igniting that concerned me. The house was a lost cause but Robbie was fighting on nevertheless, and I realised he had the same concerns. Hoisting the heavy hose over his shoulder, he was struggling with the oppressive heat. What little water there was barely made any difference.

I ran towards him.

'Stay back, Debra. It's too danger-ous.'

I felt so helpless!

Spotting some large hessian sacks just inside the open shed door, I decided to grab one. There were tiny fires in the dried dead leaves on the periphery of the clearing. Chris joined me with his own sack, flaying the sparks and tiny flames with the hessian or stamping them out with his police-issue boots when he could. From time to time we each glimpsed Robbie's unceas-ing battle with the main fire. Then, with a loud, reverberating crash, sheets of corrugated roofing fell, collapsing and crushing the flimsy partition walls inside. More fuel caused additional smoke and flames to surge up again. A gas bottle on the far side exploded with a deafen-ing roar!

Chris tapped me on the shoulder as I strained to continue beating spot fires into submission, every muscle aching.

'Cavalry's arrived. Take a break,

Debra. You need it.'

I staggered towards him, my legs too tired to keep me standing. He caught me, leading me to sit in his car. I wiped my hand across my forehead. His own face and clothing were smeared with dirt and soot, as was mine. The sweat and carbon on the back of my hand was testament to that. As for this dress . . .

We watched as the firefighters deployed like trained soldiers, jumping from the two fire tenders and accompanying water tender. They fanned out in precise movements calling out directions to one another as they unrolled heavy-duty hoses.

Robbie gladly passed the responsibility to his volunteer team. By now, the stream of water from the rainwater tank was barely a trickle.

Now, with hoses pouring gallons of water into the heart of the flames, the fire in the house was soon extinguished. The stone chimney remained defiantly intact amid the rubble and smouldering chunks of charred wood.

Like us, Robbie was too exhausted to do anything more than gasp for breath, leaning forward with his hands on his knees. One of the firemen gave us a large bottle of water to share among us, before running off to the other side of the ruin. Water never tasted so good. After drinking, I splashed my face and the others followed suit.

'Any idea of the cause?' Chris asked Robbie.

'Jimmy was a smoker. Maybe he left a cigarette burning. Those ashtrays were pretty full, weren't they, Debra?'

I agreed. In retrospect, it was an accident waiting to happen — a lit cigarette falling onto the stained rug, perhaps.

'Robbie. Senior Sergeant. We need you over here,' one firefighter called out.

There was evidently a further development.

'You stay in the car, Debra,' Chris suggested. I suspected that, like me, he was aware of what they'd found.

The three men stepped over charred timbers and shattered window glass, making their way to a fourth bloke bent over an object I could only glimpse. He'd carefully set aside beams, using gloved hands. Whatever was there would still be very hot.

As another bit of the building was pushed aside, Robbie retched. Chris peered down before stepping away. He made his way slowly back to me, head bowed.

I stepped from the car as he approached.

'Is that . . . ?' My voice was subdued and I could feel my body trembling.

'Jimmy? Looks that way. He would have died long before we arrived. You saw how bad it was. Smoke inhalation would have got him before the flames. There was nothing any of us could have done to save him.'

10

It was a sobering evening for us all. Even a long, hot bath didn't improve my disposition. Although my only meeting with Jimmy had been acrimonious, there was no way I could wish for him, or anyone, to die like that.

Chris confirmed that enough charred documents and an engraved watch had been retrieved to verify that it was Jimmy who was the deceased. Heat-cracked bottles of beers had been found at the side of the corpse. Drunk, asleep, discarded ciggy . . . that was a lethal combination.

Wendy phoned Robbie at his home to check how he was. There wasn't anything I could say to ease his pain — quite frankly, I didn't know him well enough. Any words would have been mere platitudes.

Wendy and Chris told me that they

had their own concerns about the changes in Jimmy's temperament. Later, Wendy had a private word with me . . .

'Robbie stayed by Jimmy long after everyone else gave up. But even he had reservations. Heaven knows how many times he's attempted to turn his friend's life around — especially with the gambling. He suggested to us only last week that some people are simply past helping, and I think he finally realised that Jimmy was one.'

There was something I recalled.

'Jimmy had a twin brother, up in Sydney. Robbie mentioned that he'd met him once.'

'Bill? Yeah, Chris and I had him over for a meal. Heather had just started school. Chris has already asked the New South Wales police to visit him with the news. Next of kin need to be informed in person. Jimmy was divorced so Bill's the only relative left.'

A small brandy was offered to help us get some sleep. Normally I wouldn't touch the stuff but tonight was definitely an acceptable time to make an exception.

★ ★ ★

Robbie wasn't working at the school the following day. To be fair, most of the upgrade was already complete. There was some tidying up before the system could be checked and signed off by the authorities — honest ones this time.

The temporary alarms were gone, leaving the new hard-wired ones fully functional.

I explained the situation to Ken, then went on to inform him that I was only too thrilled to accept his invitation to appoint me as Deputy Head. Seeing what had happened to poor Jimmy convinced me that I should seize any opportunity which passed my way.

We decided to keep my promotion on the QT for the present.

Weather-wise, the forecast wasn't good. The prediction was for a heat-wave with strong, gusting westerlies.

Staff and students alike were discussing it. We all realised the dreadful implications of another Black Tuesday. Many of Tassie's towns and cities were vulnerable as they had vegetation all around. Even Hobart with the Derwent on its east had the heavily wooded Mount Wellington towering above its western suburbs. Any fire would race down its slopes like a freight train, devastating everything in its path.

So far this summer, we'd been lucky, very lucky, and we all prayed it would remain so.

★　★　★

That evening, Robbie came around to the Powells. Assuming that it was Wendy he wanted to speak to, I made my excuses. There were lessons I needed to tidy up ready for my replacement, Alison, at the beginning of the following week.

'Hold up, Debra. I was wondering if you might come with me.'

Yesterday, he'd made the same request. It hadn't ended well, especially for Jimmy. And now he wanted me to go there again. I could see it in his drawn expression.

'Please, Debra. I can't do this alone.'

It was an earnest appeal, one I couldn't ignore. That bath to relax my still aching muscles would have to wait. What I found most surprising was that this strong, independent man was asking for emotional help — from me. Was that to be the relationship between us? Yin and yang, him physically capable and me supporting him mentally?

The opposite applied to me, I realised. My limits had been sorely tested yesterday yet Robbie showed no signs of fatigue or pain, at least not with his body.

'Just let me change, Robbie. I've ruined enough decent clothes over the past few weeks. Any more and I'll have to walk around naked.'

Robbie and Wendy were aghast. Then I understood what I'd said. Foot in mouth syndrome, big time.

'Well we can't have you doing that,

can we? Think of the sunburn.' Wendy giggled, breaking the difficult silence. Robbie stood there mutely. I looked down at his feet on the floor then turned and scurried off.

'Stupid, stupid, stupid,' I muttered, mentally kicking myself. Was that a Freudian slip? If so, it was totally the wrong moment.

★ ★ ★

Freshly changed into my jeans and a long-sleeved checked blouse, I re-joined Robbie. We drove out in silence, each with our own things in mind. The reek of the blackened remains permeated the air as we arrived at the still-intact shed and what was left of the house.

I stood idly by, waiting for Robbie to do whatever he needed to do. He stumbled gingerly around the wreckage, searching for I-didn't-know-what. Jimmy's body had been removed. Even the birds were quiet.

It was then that I remembered

Wendy's prediction about fire. I'd completely set it aside from my mind until this moment. Despite the warmth of the sunshine, I felt a frisson of fear run through me.

More to shake myself out of my own morbid thoughts than to discover the answer, I broke the silence by saying, 'Robbie. Have they caught up with Jimmy's brother?'

'Bill? No. Out of town. His neighbours told the Sydney cops when they called round. Does a lot of business trips, I believe. Never married but quite well off. He and Jimmy weren't close but it's only right that he's informed. I imagine he'll come down for the burial.'

'Not cremated?' I blurted out, insensitively, then caught myself. 'Sorry.'

Robbie smiled at my faux pas. He was a very tolerant man.

'Firemen never want cremation, Debra. I understand that's what in fact happened, but his remains will be buried. Jimmy discussed it with me once and I'm respecting those wishes. He named me executor. Not much to leave, apart from the land and shed here and his car.' He paused, scanning the area in all directions. 'His car . . . it's not here. Not worth much. Strange though. He must have driven here in it, yet it's nowhere to be seen.'

His attention came back to what would happen next. 'He did have some insurance so the funeral will be paid for, at least. As for the rest of his savings, I reckon he gambled that away.'

'Might his car be in the shed?' I inquired. I'd grabbed the sacks yesterday from the entrance but had never peered inside.

'If it is, that'd be a first. Jimmy never bothered to look after it, even when he worked as a builder. To him a car was something to get you from one place to another, nothing more. We'll check it out before we leave, just in case.'

Robbie was wearing heavy duty boots and gloves, as was I. The pair he'd given me were too large but they'd do. He was intent on searching the building for

Jimmy's prized possessions, war medals and that service plaque I'd seen hanging over the fireplace.

Carefully, we climbed over the precarious rubble. The chimney and fireplace stood intact and relatively unscathed though blackened with soot. There was also a peculiar odour, one which I recalled from years ago, but I couldn't identify it.

'The medals were on the stone mantelpiece in an old Arnott's bikkie box. Best place in the house, Jimmy reckoned. He was proud of them. Can you help me search? Just be careful and watch out for nails in the wood.'

Just like my dad and loads of other Aussies, Jimmy had his precious possessions in an old tin. We used to buy them full of biscuits for a Christmas treat, then keep the tin with its iconic picture of a parrot eating a cracker on the top.

There was no sign of it anywhere near the stone chimney. None of the firemen or police would have taken it and, as there was ash where the objects had been only the day before, the only

216

conclusion was that they must have been taken before the fire.

It was then that the strange smell I'd noticed before returned. We'd been moving things around.

'Can you smell that?' I asked Robbie.

'No. Told you before my sense of smell is rubbish. An accident, the doctors told Mum, when I was young. What's it like?'

I thought hard how to describe it. It reawakened a memory from my own childhood. Some sort of hydrocarbon, like petrol. There was a heater in my dad's office at the hospital — a Fireside heater. What was the fuel it used? Why couldn't I think of its name?

Then it hit me. A blue liquid . . .

'Kerosene. Yeah. Definitely kerosene.'

Robbie dropped the charred beam he was moving, narrowly missing his foot.

'What is it?' I said to him.

'This is arson, Debra. Someone stole Jimmy's keepsakes and then set the place alight.'

I put two and two together or at least

tried to — maths was not my strong point.

'Maybe Jimmy was already sleeping when the thief broke in or . . . or do you think maybe this arsonist hurt Jimmy and then set the fire? In any case, this is . . .'

'Murder,' Robbie exclaimed, his expression becoming extremely stern.

⋆ ⋆ ⋆

Obviously, Chris was soon appraised of this development. Poor Jimmy. Wrong place at the wrong time. Jimmy's gun and car were missing. Was the culprit this same arsonist who'd been terrorising the area?

My visions of a quiet life in the countryside were turning out to be anything but. It dawned on me that drama and disasters seemed to be hounding me. Since I'd begun teaching at All Saints there had been two fires.

Was I a human firestorm, after all?

Wendy told me 'No' very adamantly,

218

when I checked with her.

'It's just coincidence, Debra.'

It was then that I reminded her of a statement she'd categorically made soon after we met. 'There's no such thing,' she'd insisted. Wendy shrugged her shoulders, wiped her glasses on a hanky then gave me a weak smile.

★   ★   ★

Tuesday saw a revelation when Ken entered my empty classroom. There were documents to sign — lots of them. My mouth opened and stayed open for several seconds when I examined my new pay scale. It was double my present salary!

None of the other staff had yet been informed of the promotion although I was aware of speculation about our meetings.

'How are the remedial classes going at lunchtimes?' Ken asked.

'Encouraging. There are seven students, all keen to progress. They're a

219

wonderful support for one another and I've adopted an informal approach to them while they're there. Reading and spelling have improved noticeably. Even Mary Diamondaris is speaking up without prompting.'

She had been one of the school's quiet-as-a-mouse students when I'd first met her. These days, her confidence was beginning to bloom.

'Pleased to hear that, Debra. My own observations are most pleasing.'

There was a question I felt I must ask.

'Why the special interest, Ken?'

He paused, ruffling his hair a little, and then staring at his interlocked fingers resting on my teacher's desk.

'Guilt. I was the teacher who let these kids down when we were all in the primary school across the road . . .'

Ken started to explain, leaving me feeling like a priest listening to a long overdue confession.

As Deputy in All Saints Primary, he'd had full time responsibilities as a teacher in addition to running the school. The Principal had been as much use as, in Ken's words, a pram for a mother kangaroo. Wendy had previously mentioned her own experiences with this person when Heather had attended Primary. Her description of the Headmaster there had included a number of words that would make a wharfie blush. 'Waste of perfectly good oxygen' was the least offensive term she'd chosen to describe him.

Ken had effectively run the school, which had been rife with staffing problems. Consequently, he'd spent much of each school day literally firefighting crises with barely capable teachers, long-term illness of staff and unreliable relief. He'd had to take up the slack, spending much of his own teaching time elsewhere. His students' learning suffered. Alison had just had a baby so there'd been no assistance there.

His outpouring of this culpability indicated his level of belief that I could assist his former students to reach their potential and make All Saints a school to be proud of. It was humbling but gave me that much more incentive to work with him as a progressive team.

★ ★ ★

Returning to the Powells' after school, I saw that Chris was already home. He'd be on duty again later that evening. His unmarked car was at the side of the house.

Wendy and Heather were specks on the horizon, tending to the herd — or 'beasties' as Wendy called them — in one of the paddocks.

Before I realised it, another car appeared on the long drive, approaching where I was standing. I groaned. It was that unfaithful cane-toad, Shane! He clearly couldn't take a hint even if it were delivered with a chunk of four-by-four hardwood. It was evident that he'd followed me, albeit discreetly, from school.

There was no point prolonging the

meeting so I stood, arms folded. Unfortunately, that meant a cloud of dust enveloped me as he screeched to a halt. I was not a happy bunny.

Shane stepped out, oblivious to the if-looks-could-kill stare I was giving him. As he walked over to me I wondered what I'd ever seen in him.

'I've decided to give you one final last chance, Debs. You can come back to me — I've forgiven you for leaving me.'

Bearing in mind I was determined not to be upset by his unwanted presence, I tried to keep my cool.

'How generous of you, Shane. The answer remains 'No'. And in case you don't understand English too well, despite once being an English teacher, I shall translate for you . . . non, that's French . . . niet, Russian . . . nein, German . . . nihil, Latin . . . oh, and bugger off. That last one is Australian, just for you.'

'There's no need to be like that, Debs. Not if you want some of that money back,' Shane teased, nastily.

'Some of . . . ?' I began, seething.

Just in time, I heard the fly-screen door hinges squeak. Chris appeared at the front door, dressed in lime green shorts and long socks. The shirt was one of those horrid Hawaiian ones like the baddies wore in Hawaii Five-0. There should have been a law against wearing such a combination in public, especially in Tassie.

On this occasion, however, I wasn't bothered.

'Problems, Debra?' he said, strolling up the sloping path to us.

'Who's this then, Debs?' Shane sneered.

He attempted to look tough, ignoring the gaudy but quietly confident man before him. At that point, Shane took a deep breath, puffing his chest out like some demented emu.

'Wait. Let me guess . . . you're Debra's new lover and that's why she's shacked up with you.'

Chris said nothing but I did detect a sly smile. He remained passive and relaxed.

I could learn a lot from his self-control. I imagined he'd met his share of aggressive men. My former boyfriend would never learn when it was wise to back down or how to pick his fights. But Shane wasn't finished.

'Bloody hell, Debs. I suspected you were into father figures, but I thought you could do better than this pensioner!'

That did it. Insulting me was one thing, but to have a go at my friends was bang out of order!

'Says you, the lying schmuck who cheated on me and stole from me!' I shot back.

Chris reacted, making a move forward. Shane stepped back, his smile vanishing in an instant. Yet Chris was still calm as a cucumber on LSD.

'Oh, so you're Shane Pendleton, the bloke who stole Debra's money and lost his job. Pleased to meet you, Shane.'

Chris extended his hand which Shane stupidly took, and then winced in pain as Chris closed his hand firmly and held Shane in its grip.

'I'm the owner of this property, mate. Me and my wife over there.' He pointed up towards the paddocks. 'Debra's staying with us as a boarder, and we've heard all about you, Shane.'

My ex tried desperately to extract his hand from Chris' vice-like grip. I could see the sweat on his forehead and his bared teeth.

'I also happen to be a Senior Sergeant with the Tassie police, and I couldn't help but notice what a great car you have there . . . what say you and me have a good squizz at it, man to . . . well, man? Mind if I call you Shanie? After all Debra told us about you, I reckon we're best of mates now.'

At that point, he released Shane's poor, broken hand. Chris peeked in the open window of the Holden Torana.

'Hmm. Bit of a tip in there, Shanie-boy. Seat belt is damaged — that's actually illegal. Well then, let's see what other defects we can find with this fine car of yours . . . ' Shane cringed a little. 'Not to worry, Shanie-boy, we're mates, remember? Mind you, those tyres look pretty bald to me. Not good at all, even if we are best buddies. Still, that's no problem, especially as you said you're returning all Debra's money today.'

Shane was indignant. 'Me? Give her money? I never said that.'

'Didn't you? Sorry, Shanie. Us pensioners are a bit deaf. Never mind, what say I just ask one of my fellow officers to have a look over this beaut car of yours. Probably give you a few points — oh, and a fine, no doubt.

'Come to that, I did notice an empty can of Cascade and your breath stinks a bit . . . have you been drinking? I'm not sure Shanie-boy, but we can check if you like?'

By this time, Shane was quite pale.

Chris still wasn't finished toying with him, though, and went on, 'About Debra's money. A cheque would be all right, I reckon.'

Shane knew he was beaten.

Reluctantly, he retrieved his cheque book from the glove box of the car, completing it as per our instructions. I took it from his shaking hand before he could change his mind.

'Off you go now, Shanie. I don't want to see you in The Valley again . . . understand?'

He offered his hand again, but Shane was already in his car and starting the engine.

We waved him farewell.

'Who was that?' Wendy asked, as she arrived.

Chris replied, 'No one important.'

I left them with a spring in my step, clutching the cheque — but not before giving Chris a 'thank you' hug!

As I skipped off, I heard Wendy observe with a cheeky tone. 'If Debra reacts that way for 'nothing', mister, I'd best keep my eye on you!'

★ ★ ★

Following tea that evening, Chris told me that Jimmy's brother, Bill, had been in contact with the Cronulla police in Sydney. He was flying down on the weekend.

Jimmy's body was in the care of the coroner. Considering it was now a suspicious death, an autopsy was underway.

'Any clues as to the arsonist's identity — assuming there's just the one?'

I scooped another spoonful of ice cream with passionfruit topping into my mouth. Wendy was also enjoying a dish of ice cream, helping me celebrate getting Shane's cheque.

'Just the one. Red Cap was noticed near Jimmy's place. He was driving away about twenty minutes before we arrived.'

Later, when Chris and Heather were working on her homework, Wendy produced my progression astrology chart.

'Venus in the Eighth House means unexpected but deserved wealth. That

— ahem — change at work, perhaps? As I said, it's all happening for you this week. There's even love out there for you, if you want it.'

'Love? Don't suppose it says who it will be? Tall, dark and handsome?'

She gave me a grin. 'The stars aren't that prescriptive, Debra. And the future isn't definite. All I can say is that there is someone who can be special in your life. You're always in control of your destiny, though. Never forget that.'

In a way, that was comforting, and the next morning when I woke and looked outside, Venus was shining brightly in the pre-dawn sky. The planet was named after the Roman goddess of love and, at this time of the year, it was quite prominent. Depending on the month, it was often called either the Morning or the Evening Star, though it wasn't a star at all.

I gazed upward, musing.

'What surprises do you have for me, please?'

There was no answer which was

hardly surprising. A teeny-weeny whispered hint would have been appreciated though.

★ ★ ★

During my next day at school, I went down the road during a free period to bank the cheque with my 'new-found wealth'. There was also the school mail to be taken to the post office. One less job for our hard-pressed secretaries.

Agnes was tending the counter, and I was the only customer. 'G'day,' I greeted her.

After sorting out the mail with her, I was about to leave when she stopped me, saying she had some important facts to tell me about Robbie Sanderson.

My ears pricked up but I kept my cool.

'Yes, I've met him. He's an electrician. Been working at the school.'

One thing I'd decided early on was to keep my personal life private. There was no way I wanted to be the subject of local gossip — not if there was anything I could do about it.

'Yeah. Now that Sam's retired, I guess he's the only 'leckie hereabouts. Nonetheless, there's something you should be aware of — you and him being single and all . . .'

'Go on, Agnes,' I prompted her, warily.

Was Agnes aware we were close? Possibly. We'd been seen together a few times, in and out of school. At least one local mother I recognised by face if not by name had spotted us together at Wrest Point. After that tongues may have wagged.

Agnes leaned forward as though she were sharing a confidence.

'I don't trust that man.' That was a surprise. Agnes continued. 'You're a strong, intelligent woman, Debra, and maybe he behaves different around you, but all I know for certain is no one around here has any confidence in the man, not after his conviction.'

'Conviction for what?'

'Armed robbery. He even did time in

prison. I'd keep my distance from that bloke if I was you, Debra.' She stood back as a young mum with a pram and toddler pushed open the fly-screen door. I chose to leave, pondering her words.

While I could not accept her revelation at face value, I couldn't ignore it either. Armed robbery? It was then and there that I decided I'd avoid getting too close to Robbie Sanderson, as much as I enjoyed his company. My brain was beginning to ache from too much thinking about Robbie's past. It was a good thing I had a busy remainder of the day teaching.

★   ★   ★

Robbie was with Wendy when I arrived home late that afternoon. He was dressed in his firefighter's gear which was covered in mud and debris. Another brush fire to contend with, no doubt. The following week would test him and his team to their limits.

'Hi Debra. Wendy just gave me the

233

great news about your promotion.'

I shot a dirty glance at Wendy. It was supposed to be a secret. Robbie must have noticed.

'Hey, don't worry, Debra. Wendy believed it'd be fine to tell just me. As for keeping quiet about it, you can trust me. You do know that, don't you?'

Did I? That was my first thought. Before I could respond, Robbie asked me to go to the pictures in Huonville on Saturday night.

'*The Exorcist.* You told me you like creepy movies. Unless you've already seen it, Debra?'

'I . . . I saw it last year in Hobart. Sorry. You should go, though, it's good. I've a lot of school prep to do on Saturday night anyway — new job and all that.'

The disappointment was clear in his eyes.

I made my own excuses and left him and Wendy discussing the threat of fires near us.

It wasn't much later that I heard

Wendy's footsteps on the lino in the hall. She knocked, and entered when I invited her in.

Her anger was evident.

'That was so rude, Debra. You told me only last week you were keen to see that movie.'

I glanced up from my marking book.

'I thought you two were getting on like a house on fire — oh, bad choice of words, but you know what I mean. You two were close. What happened?'

I tried to calm her.

'Nothing's happened. I just have a lot on my mind. You of all people should understand that.'

'What? Because I used to teach? No, Debra. That won't wash. Whatever reasons you have, I must respect. But I'm disappointed in you. That's a shame because I thought we were friends.'

She closed the door leaving me to ponder over her words. We *were* friends. I'd wanted to tell her that, but the expression on her face had upset me too much. In retrospect, I'd reacted badly, behaving like a spoilt schoolgirl.

Agnes was a stranger whose words had changed my feelings far more than they should have. Hearing Wendy's footsteps on the gravel outside, I decided to try and resolve this upset as best I could. I stood up to follow her. She'd probably gone to help Heather with the beasts.

The sun was hot as I headed outside to where I could hear raised voices.

Someone was screaming — it was Heather!

Dashing past an outbuilding, I could see my student gasping for air. Wendy was panicking.

Then I saw the cause of the distress . . .

Jack jumper ants! They were everywhere, making the ground look like a heaving sea. Somehow Heather had been bitten and was showing signs of anaphylactic shock. Without rapid intervention that darling girl would die!

11

Sprinting forward, I grabbed Heather around the waist, carrying her well away from the surging sea of ants. Wendy ran after me, realising the cause of Heather's dire predicament.

Carefully, I put her down on a clear area and began to pull her trousers off — the obnoxious black ants with orange pincers were attached to her legs and one on her tummy.

Wendy was screaming, too. It was then that I understood she'd also been stung. She frantically pulled her own jeans off, brushing the insidious insects from her calves and thighs.

Already her legs were red and swollen.

She tugged her jeans over her boots and shook them vigorously, ants flung away.

My own concerns were for Heather.

She was in intense pain, crying as she struggled to breathe.

These ants were notorious in Tassie — aggressive and able to leap vast distances, they fixed their mandibles into the flesh before twisting their bodies to sting with their tails.

'Heather — has she been attacked before?' I asked her mum. Wendy wasn't thinking straight. 'Quickly, Wendy.'

'Er . . . yes, but not like this.'

'She's in serious trouble. Anaphylaxis. Allergic reaction. Throat's swelling. Get her inside.'

We must have looked bizarre, all unclothed. This was no time for shyness. Together we carried Heather to the house. Once there, I told Wendy to call an ambulance. I hurried to my room where I had some adrenalin and syringes in an Ana-kit. Heather was worse when I came back. I scanned the dosage chart. 'Adrenalin. What's her weight?'

Wendy realised the importance of the correct dosage. I filled the syringe to the correct mark then dabbed iodine on

Heather's upper leg.

'Do you know what you're doing, Debra? If anything happens . . . '

'My dad's a surgeon. He trained me to use this. I'm allergic to the little buggers, too.'

'Oh hell. You weren't stung, were you?'

'No.' If I had, I'd be in agony too. 'Your call, Wendy. We can wait for the ambos . . . ?'

We both knew that Heather didn't have time to wait. Her face was starting to swell.

Wendy took my hand. 'Go on. Do it.'

I plunged the needle into the part of the thigh with the antiseptic iodine wash, praying it would work. For ages we watched, until at last her laboured breathing gradually slowed.

'It's working, isn't it, Debra?'

Heather's eyes opened. 'Mum? Miss Winters?'

'Those ants, sweetheart. They must have gotten through your clothing.'

She must have been standing on a nest.

In the distance, there was a siren. The ambulance would take her to Hobart for checks. Tragedy averted — this time.

★ ★ ★

At the hospital, Heather was given the all-clear. The American doctor told us the epinephrine administered early had done the job.

'I thought it was adrenalin.' Wendy held Heather's hand as she lay in bed, appearing much better.

'Same stuff, different word, Mrs Powell. You wouldn't believe how hard it is to learn Aussie. So many differences from English or American.'

They were keeping Heather in overnight, so it was time to drive back to the Huon. By then, it was dark. Chris had already poured petrol down the nest entrance. The fumes would kill the ants off. He'd bring in pest exterminators later.

I offered to drive on the tricky roads

around Fern Tree but Wendy said she was all right. We sat in her car, taking a moment before setting off.

It was time for me to explain.

'I apologise for earlier, Wendy. Someone told me horrible things about Robbie, and it was brainless of me to believe them.'

In the dim light of the car, I noticed Wendy's surprised features.

'Listen. Robbie was no angel back then. Joy-riding, vandalism . . .'

'Armed robbery? Prison?'

'What the . . . ?' She shook her head. 'I can understand your reticence to go out with Robbie now, but I can tell you that it's a lie, a horrible, vindictive lie.' She clenched her hands around the steering wheel. 'Who told you this, Debra?'

'A woman in the post office near school. Agnes someone.' I mentally kicked myself for not trusting my own instincts.

Wendy gave a sharp intake of breath. 'Not Agnes O'Rourke? Damn it,

Debra. Didn't you know that her hubby is the electrician who first did the school alarms?'

I felt so gullible! Agnes had played me like a fool, and this was her revenge.

I punched the dashboard in anger. It hurt.

'Debra, I told you that one of your astrological flaws was being too trusting.'

'That bloody cow!' I blurted out, ashamed of myself for being so gullible, as much as for the bad language of my reaction!

Wendy reached over to massage my hand.

'Don't worry, Debra. Now we know who the culprit is, we can have our payback.'

In the meantime, I had to give Robbie a ring and apologise. Watching *The Exorcist* by myself wasn't an option anyway, and I did want to see it.

★ ★ ★

I once read that revenge was a dish best served cold. It was a strange saying, inferring that you shouldn't rush into using firey emotions straight away but stick them in the fridge for a bit.

Agnes had tried to besmirch Robbie's reputation. Unfortunately, my inner mind wanted to lash out at her immediately.

That night, I kept tossing around in bed, unable to sleep. When the Sandman came to whisk me off to Dreamland, he stuck me in some horrid nightmare with a bushfire all around. It howled through the undergrowth and tree canopies with the shriek of banshees and laughing faces of orange and blood-red.

A man in an asbestos suit came lumbering through the flames.

'You have to hide, Debra. Hide where they can't see you!'

I could feel my skin blistering from the inferno's heat, singeing my hair, scorching my clothing. Their faces danced, stretching and vanishing, only to reappear elsewhere.

'Where? Where can I hide?' I demanded.

'Somewhere they can't reach you!'

He lowered his head, scratching at the ground with his protected foot. Then he vanished in a fireball. I woke in a sweat, my heart racing and my mouth bone-dry. What did it all mean?

★ ★ ★

The morning meeting in the school staff room was the start of a memorable day.

Ken called for everyone's attention.

'Ladies and gentlemen. In light of the very welcome increased enrolment of pupils, we need — or rather I need — a Deputy Head more than ever. Consequently, I have appointed Miss Debra Winters to the position, effective next week.'

There were a number of enthusiastic claps and shouted congratulations, with Doris's cheers being the most vocal.

Smiling, I thanked my fellow staff. The secretaries were there too. From an initial awkwardness between us when I'd arrived, we were now friends. All but one there was pleased for me. When Martin Day spoke up, it was evident he was seething.

'How can you do that, Ken? Debra's barely older than a child herself. She's still a novice. On the other hand, I have seniority and experience and I deserve to have that job. Besides, she's a sheila. The students of All Saints would never respect a woman in authority.'

Although Ken had warned me this might happen, it was still disconcerting. I glared at Martin who avoided my gaze.

Ken had told me he'd deal with Martin and he did. After all, it was Ken's decision that was under challenge.

'Martin, your chauvinism does you no justice. I have the full support of the parents in my choice as well as Chief Office. Furthermore, you're ready for

245

retirement — one more year, you told me. This position would only be a means to boost your pension and that is not the sort of motivation I need in my Deputy. All Saints needs a dedicated leader, not a caretaker.'

However, Martin wasn't finished.

'You better change your mind, Ken. Otherwise I'll . . . I'll have to resign.'

'I'm not altering my decision, Martin. I will be sad to see you go. Shall we give you a week in lieu of proper notice?'

Martin's ruddy face suddenly drained of colour. We all watched him, waiting for a retraction, but his male pride meant he had to go through with his foolish threat.

'So be it, Ken. You'll be sorry, though. Anyone else resigning over this?'

No one moved. His exit from the staff room was embarrassing to watch.

Ken turned to me. 'Looks like we need a new science teacher, Debra. Anyone in mind?'

Martin going like that was a shock to us all. Nevertheless, I knew there was a possible replacement in mind.

'Leave it with me, Ken,' I replied as confidently as I could with fingers crossed behind my back.

* * *

We'd offered to collect Bill Jordan from the airport but he'd told Robbie and me that all was sorted since he'd arranged a car hire and was intent on staying in Hobart at some swish hotel.

From what I'd gathered, Bill could afford it. Robbie had met him some years earlier prior to Jimmy commencing his downward spiral into a shadow of the man he'd once been. At that time Jimmy was chief of the local firefighters with Robbie as his friend and deputy. Jimmy had still been married then. Even so, Robbie was keen to elucidate on the differences between the twins.

'Meeting the two of them, I reckoned they weren't even related. Bill had a three-piece suit on. Jimmy wouldn't have been seen dead in one of them.'

Robbie bit his lip. He'd realised the slip with the dead comment too late.

My friend had suggested the Bushranger Hotel in Huonville. There wasn't a large choice of public places around here. The usual cream tiles that adorned the outside of many Aussie pubs, were here too. In my opinion the decor was far more suited to a men's toilet but then again, it wasn't the sort of place most ladies would frequent.

We were sat in the so-called Ladies Lounge on some seats and benches that had once been covered in an emerald green velvet but were now threadbare in many places. Flypaper rolls dangled from the ceiling, dotted with insects that had become stuck and died there.

Robbie and I were the only two there, each sipping a beer. Through the open door to the main bar, we could hear the raucous din of men drinking and laughing as they watched some Aussie Rules match from Melbourne on a black and white telly. In two or three years, they were planning on bringing colour television to Australia but I reckoned most people couldn't afford it so it'd be a waste of time and money.

Progress was slow in Tassie. One day women might be allowed to join the blokes in the main bar, but for the foreseeable future, us 'sheilas' were confined to places like this in most Aussie hotels. I suspected the real reason was the rampant chauvinism. No doubt they'd be swearing, telling crude jokes and ogling the semi-clad women on the calendars or behind the bar. Yep, women were allowed in the all-male bar when it suited them all right.

'You OK, Debra? We still on for the flicks later?'

'Sure. Looking forward to being scared out of my wits. I was just wondering if you and Bill would be better in there with other blokes instead of here. It's not exactly the Ritz — or Wrest Point.'

'Bill suggested meeting up with you

249

too when I mentioned what happened. As for me, I prefer the company of a beautiful woman these days.'

Wendy and I had told him what had happened with Agnes. She wouldn't be spreading her rumours any more. In fact, she'd been very apologetic.

It transpired that her hubby, Sam, had been economical with the truth. He'd said he retired because Robbie had been bad-mouthing him. When Wendy had explained about the school alarms being defective, she'd been horrified that Sam had been so crooked. Agnes wanted to make up for her lies to me by now recommending Robbie as the new electrician.

'Anyway, Bill can only spare a few days here,' Robbie was saying. 'To meet us, see where Jimmy died, and pay his respects. They hadn't been close but family is family.'

'He's not staying for the funeral?'

'No. Off to Brissie on Monday then onto Tokyo. Some sort of financial consultant or something. Funeral might be a while, since the autopsy confirmed it was murder.'

I put my hand on Robbie's. 'I wanted to apologise again.'

He gave a warm, reassuring grin. 'No need. Just so long as you don't think I'm some evil master criminal.' He took his hand away to sip his drink and didn't put it back on mine. Instead he adjusted his shirt collar. Once again, I assumed he'd been reminded of his dark past.

I held the ice-cold glass of beer to my forehead. It was sweltering in here, even with the fans on.

'Aren't you hot with that heavy shirt on?'

I wore a thin sleeveless frock and even the blokes in the bar had navy blue or white singlets on, exposing their muscled arms and beer bellies as well as the occasional hairy navel!

In retrospect, Robbie was over-dressed. Perhaps it was in deference to meeting a proper gentleman like Bill. Perhaps it was for my benefit. Who knew what went on in his thoughts?

Through the main bar door, a big, tubby guy entered. Robbie jumped up to shake his hand.

'Bill — over here.'

'Robbie — and this lovely lass must be your girlfriend. Diana, isn't it?' He shook my hand.

'Debra. I'm just Robbie's friend, not girlfriend.'

'Fancy a drink, Bill?' Robbie asked.

'Pepsi. Lots of ice — and another of whatever you two are having.'

Bill reached into his wallet and produced a fifty-dollar bill. I'd never seen one before! Then he sat opposite me, patting his bulging tummy. He was so different to Jimmy, immaculate hair, peppered with grey. And he must have been twenty pounds or more heavier.

The main difference was his presence, though. I could see why he was a successful businessman. He took his time examining the room, brushing a fleck off his tie as he did so.

'Not what you're used to, Mr Jordan?'

'Call me Bill, please.' He smiled. 'No, it's not, but I've seen much worse. In Ceylon there were gaps in the floor-boards so large I was afraid I'd fall through. And the stench! This establishment is a touch of paradise in comparison. But nowhere near as impressive as Raffles over in George Town, Malaysia. However, my roots were in places like this . . . me and Jimmy.'

He loosened his silk tie, undid the cuff-links and rolled up the sleeves of his shirt. His fingernails were neatly trimmed and his glowing face clean shaven. Unlike Jimmy he had all his teeth, though still yellowed from tobacco.

Robbie returned with the drinks and change.

'You sure you don't want a beer, Bill? You could have mine.'

Bill gave a full-bellied laugh. 'No thank you, young man. I never touch a drop. Rots the brain.' He noticed our reaction, then added hastily, 'If imbibed to excess, of course.'

The businessman leaned forward.

'I'm pleased to have met you both today. It's an opportunity to thank you personally for trying to save Jimmy from that dreadful death. Though, to be honest, Jimmy was lost to me years ago. We are — were — twins and there is that genetic link. There, but for the whims of the gods, I could have been that sad reprobate who squandered his reputation, marriage and life on demon drink and gambling.'

Three men entered the lounge, large glasses in their hands. They were trying to be sombre, though I thought them rather too drunk to be sincere.

'You Jimmy's brother?' one asked. Considering he was an identical twin, the point was moot. 'Just wanted to pay our respects. He was a bonza bloke, he was.'

Bill stood to shake their hands as introductions were made. 'Thank you all. A pleasure to meet Jimmy's mates.' He took another fifty from his wallet. 'Tell you what, fellas. Take this back to the bar and give everyone a shout to celebrate Jimmy's life.'

'A fifty?' one of them exclaimed. 'That'd give him a proper send-off!'

Bill accompanied them to the bar. It was a magnanimous gesture. A loud shout erupted from the other room. He'd made a few new friends, it seemed. Upon his return he drained his own glass while standing.

'Nice blokes. Salt of the earth. Shall we go out to Jimmy's old place in my car? You'll have to navigate, Robbie.'

'Your car? Might get a bit dirty,' said Robbie.

'No worries. I prefer a touch of luxury when I travel. Doubt your car has air-conditioning and it is damn hot. Pardon my French, Debra.'

Outside the sun was scorching, even with hats and sunnies on.

Bill's car was a large Mercedes-Benz.

'Front seat or back, Miss Winters?'

'Back, thanks. You and Robbie can have a chat. Besides, he knows the way. Jimmy's shack was quite isolated.'

As we drove, I relaxed back in the

plush seats, a far cry from the Bushranger. Even the windows were tinted. My focus drifted to the scenery rather than the muffled conversation from up front.

The beer helped me appreciate the Tassie scenery. Because the weather here was so much dryer than British countryside, many immigrants found fault with the paler, dried-out green of our native vegetation. Nevertheless, it was beautiful to me. Sparse leaves wafted in the hot breezes, shining in the sunlight. I loved rural Tasmania. Here, far from the oppressive, unnatural buildings and roads of Hobart, I felt as though this was where I belonged.

Thinking about Robbie, I berated my short-lived distrust of him. He'd been the perfect gentleman and showed all the qualities I admired in a potential partner. His sense of humour mirrored my own, his rugged good looks and engaging personality made him an ideal man to me. I had no doubt that the hero in my dreams was Robbie.

Was I falling in love with Robbie on the rebound? I had no idea. If I were, would that be so disastrous? I was young and destined to make my share of mistakes, though an inner part of me doubted this would be one of them.

What could be the worst that might happen? Another broken heart? Well, I was a big girl now, a Deputy Head in fact. Even if everyone and their dingo told me it was too early to be involved with a guy again, I thought Robbie was worth taking a chance on.

The problem, I decided, wasn't me being open to love him — it was Robbie. Every time he'd shown a hint of affection to me, something else appeared to frighten him from committing.

And it wasn't just me. Wendy had told me he hadn't been involved with women in the past. Did he lack self-confidence — or was it that being in The Valley with its constant reminders of his delinquent past, made him think he didn't deserve to be happy with a woman?

Returning to the scene of a crime wasn't easy for anyone. Although I'd hardly met poor Jimmy, I was quite concerned about Robbie's reactions.

There was always the possibility that Jimmy had been killed by the arsonist because he was once a fireman. That meant my Robbie might also be a potential target.

Stepping out from the comfort of the car was a major reminder that this was a heatwave. My hair was flung in all directions, so I fastened it into a makeshift pony-tail.

I chose to wait by the car as Robbie and Bill made their cautious way through the scattered mess to the charcoaled ruins of Jimmy's home.

Despite his outwardly stoic nature, Bill was wiping tears from his eyes. He made the sign of the cross and folded his hands to pray. I stood upright and did the same. It felt right to pay my respects too.

Eventually they walked away, Bill choosing to wander to the still intact tin shed.

'There's nothing in there, Bill,' Robbie called out. 'I've already checked.'

'Just curious about my wayward brother,' he replied. 'What his life here was like. There's nothing else of his left.'

Robbie nodded. He returned to my side where I took his hand.

We were surprised when Bill returned with an old hessian sack, covered in straw.

'It was under a pile of hay in the corner.'

He reached inside and produced the missing plaque and medals.

I spoke up. 'We wondered where they'd disappeared to, Bill. Robbie told me they were important to Jimmy. I'm glad they've turned up.'

Robbie rubbed his chin, pensively.

'I wonder why they were there? Did Jimmy move them there — or was it the killer?'

It was Bill who suggested an answer

259

that made sense.

'Maybe the arsonist was in a rush, hearing your car coming? We'll never learn the truth. In any case, I'm keeping them, to remind me of the brother I've lost.'

We left soon after that. Bill dropped us back at the pub where Robbie had his car, apologising for rushing us.

'I have to make a conference call to the board of a company in Los Angeles at seven tonight, our time. Time differences are a pain sometimes. It was really lovely to have met you both. Do enjoy your movie.'

'Our thoughts are with you, Bill,' I said.

As he left, Robbie said, 'Nice bloke. Disconcerting to see him in some ways, though. He was just like Jimmy used to be . . . before his problems started.'

'Yeah. I can imagine,' I agreed.

Something wasn't right, though, with what he'd said when he was leaving. I put it down to the upset of witnessing-the place where his brother perished, but even so ... conference calls on a Saturday? Unlikely. I reckoned he had other business to attend to in Hobart.

All that money. Was he a legitimate businessman or was he up to a shady deal tonight?

12

Before we headed off to the cinema, Robbie joined us all for an indoor barbie. To cook anything outside would have been madness, as even one spark could start a fire miles away.

Chris and Robbie were outside, laying out hoses in case there was a bushfire. Heather was sitting nearby preparing the salad, which left Wendy and I tending to the steaks and snags.

That suited me fine, as I had a proposition to put to her.

'Careful, Debra. The sausages. We want them cooked, not burned to cinders.'

I turned down the gas on the stove.

'Martin Day has resigned,' I mentioned casually as I stepped aside for Wendy to tend the steaks under the grills. 'He took the huff about my appointment.'

Wendy paused. 'That's interesting.' She wasn't making this easy. Heather listened surreptitiously as she set the table with sauces and chunks of pineapple in a covered dish.

'So, we need a replacement science teacher, and I was wondering if you would . . . ?'

Wendy picked up a knife. A sharp knife.

'If I would what, Miss Winters?'

'Well, I reckon you'd make a great teacher at All Saints. At least let me explain before you do something with that knife I might regret!'

Not that I actually thought she would, but with all that had happened, it was wise not to take chances. Glancing at the knife, she broke out into a wide grin. She dropped it into the washing-up water then dried her hands on her apron.

'Go on. You're perfectly safe now, Debra.'

I took a deep breath and spoke quickly so she couldn't interrupt with

263

an emphatic 'No' before I had finished.

'You're an accomplished teacher. The kids deserve more than reading text books, and our school has loads of mothballed equipment ready to use in practical experiments. You'd love it, the kids would love it, and you'll be able to afford to employ Hans full time. Please say yes, Wendy. Pretty please!'

Wendy glanced at Heather who was nodding enthusiastically.

'I'll think about it. There's Chris and Hans to check with. And Heather, of course. Maybe she won't like me being in the same school, teaching her. Still, talking to dumb beasts all day isn't exactly stretching my mind. But give me some time to decide.'

I said a silent triumphant 'Yes!'

Very soon I was sure that Wendy would be our new resident 'mad scientist', exploding things and making smelly sulphuric gas.

That reminded me ... Bill had a funny smell about him. I'd noticed it in the car. Some medication?

Heather came over to help her mum. She had beetroot over her apron. I smiled. Usually that was me. I'd have to be careful having tea tonight. Too many scorched or damaged clothes already this year. Time for a shopping trip next weekend? A girls' day out sounded like a great idea.

★ ★ ★

The film was scary as hell and memorable. Trouble was that, while we held hands, there were no cuddles or tender kisses from Robbie in the back row. The wee small hours saw me having more nightmares, though . . .

'You need to hide, Debra,' the dream fireman told me before vanishing in a burst of flames.

I woke up shivering, despite the heat, Venus peeking through the chink in the curtains, taunting me.

Something momentous was happening. I could sense it. Although it could have been easy to dismiss it as auto-suggestion from Wendy's whacky planetary predictions, it felt more real than that. My life these past weeks had been turned topsy-turvy and I suspected the upheaval was far from over.

An angry branch brushed against the window, blown by the restless winds. Then I heard a sound, soft and enticing like a siren's song. Was there someone outside, calling out to me?

'Get a grip, Debra Winters,' I said aloud. 'Believing in astrology and premonitions? You're a rational woman. There are no such things.'

I calmed down and eventually drifted back to sleep, though I could still hear those whispered voices from the trees as I nodded off . . . *Hide, Debra Winters. Hide!*

* * *

I was late getting ready to accompany Heather and Wendy down to the herd. I'd promised to help out and, at the same time, learn what real country life

266

was all about. Wendy was waiting outside in one of the old shearing sheds.

'Bad night,' I apologised, watching the fierce winds stir the dust into more willy-willies, our own Aussie mini-tornadoes. It was already twenty-eight degrees and it was just after eight. 'But I'm ready. Let's go and meet these cows of yours.'

When we began walking, Heather chose to explain the facts of beef farming to me.

'Actually, Miss Winters, we have steers here. They're males that have been . . . well, you know. You do understand the difference between male and female cattle, don't you?' She giggled.

Wendy added her bit. 'We have two types here. Murray Greys and Angus. And an Angus bull.'

'I do know what a bull is, thank you,' I replied.

Then I noticed a dark shape wobbling along the ground beneath some trees, before nudging a log aside to search for food. She was quite large for a wombat.

'Local friend of yours?' I asked. 'Does she have a name?'

'Wilamina,' Wendy replied.

'Katy,' said Heather at the same time.

'Two names,' I commented. 'Must be a special animal.'

Wendy paused, rather contrite. 'Actually, she's called Debbie.'

'You named a fat, hairy wombat after me?'

I wasn't sure if I should be flattered or insulted.

'She's been around for years and she's always been Debbie. It's unfortunate but I'm not changing her name — and unless you change yours, you'll just have to live with it.'

I knelt down to shake her paw. 'Pleased to meet you, Debbie. Guess that explains all those sniggers when I first turned up and told you my name. I would have understood. I just wish she wasn't so . . . so *round*.'

Heather pointed to the horizon. 'Over there.'

In the distance thin wisps of smoke

268

were barely discernible. Another fire.

Chances were, the arsonist had struck again. It was the hottest day of the year and the winds were strong. It wasn't a good omen.

★ ★ ★

Much later, we were all relaxing after lunch in the relative cool of the lounge. Chris had sprayed the outside of the house with spring water to help cool us down. The blinds were all drawn. Mad dogs and Englishmen might be out in the midday sun but we had more sense.

I was preparing lessons. Wendy was reading some new book about the joys of motherhood, it seemed, called *Rosemary's Baby*. Chris and Heather were playing Monopoly.

As for Robbie, I imagined he was out there somewhere, possibly fighting a fire. The contrast in our lazy Sunday afternoons was hard to grasp. At least there were no infernos nearby. We had the radio on for news updates.

Wendy broke the silence suddenly.

'By the way, the answer is 'Yes', Debra.'

It was a casual statement, made as she was still reading.

I was so engrossed in my own work, I didn't understand. 'Sorry, Wendy. Answer to what?'

Her eyes still never left her book. 'That job you offered me.'

My eyes lit up. I immediately put my work aside to embrace her. 'Thank you, thank you!' I said.

Chris and Heather watched us, broad grins on their faces. 'How long did it take you to decide?'

'Oh, about . . . three seconds.' She removed her glasses to mop her brow. 'It was fun seeing you sweat, though!'

'I'm doing enough of that already from this heat, thank you very much.' I took out a hanky to wipe my own forehead. 'Besides. Only horses sweat — men perspire, and we ladies glow!'

Although right now, the distinction was not worth debating. What we needed was a good old-fashioned thunderstorm to cool us all off.

Heather wandered over from the game to sit by me. 'Now you're in a good mood, Miss Winters, can I ask a favour? I have these raffle tickets from the Girl Guides. Would you buy a book, please?'

'Of course. In fact, make it five books.'

The mention of raffles had me thinking . . . Jimmy's addiction to gambling. Yet there was another memory, something Bill had said.

'Wendy. Might I check your encyclopaedia?' Most families had twenty-odd volumes of the massive collection sold by door-to-door salesmen.

'Certainly. What are you searching for?'

'Believe it or not, raffles,' I replied taking the relevant volume from a shelf. I sat down to leaf through the book. 'Ah-ha! I was right.'

Taking the open encyclopaedia to the table I ran my finger down the script. The others gathered around. 'Bill Jordan was talking about hotels he's been in. He said Raffles was in Malaysia. It's

271

not. It's in Singapore.'

Chris spoke up. 'The Eastern and Oriental is in George Town, Malaysia.' We stared at him, surprised. 'Don't look at me like that. I'm not a total dill. I know a few things more than police stuff. What does this mean, though?'

'By itself, nothing. But he also said he had a conference call to Los Angeles at seven last night. It'd be Saturday there too, so unlikely.'

Chris did some reckoning in his head. 'Seven pm Saturday here would be two o'clock in the morning Saturday there.' Once again, he surprised us with his knowledge.

'There's no way American board members would be up then. Bill was telling lies because he wanted to make me believe he was some successful businessman.' I hesitated before expressing my next words. Was I totally mad for even considering the possibility? 'I wonder if he's the real Bill, or someone just pretending.'

Chris was more alert than Wendy.

'Pretending? But who . . . surely you

can't be suggesting Jimmy. We have his body.'

'Exactly. There's a body — a body.'

It was all making sense now. The whole idea was impossible. Two twins, one rich, one poor. It would require a lot of planning and much more.

'Robbie would have noticed. Jimmy was his friend and mentor. He would have seen through Jimmy impersonating Bill.' Chris was thinking about the implications, playing Devil's advocate.

I'd wondered about that too.

'But Robbie had no reason to believe that Bill wasn't Bill. They look the same apart from hair, beard, and so on. Robbie would be seeing differences rather than similarities. And no one has verified it was Jimmy's body. No fingerprints. What about teeth?'

'I'm on it,' said Chris, leaving us to phone from the kitchen.

Then I remembered another thing . . . Bill and Jimmy had an odour about their person, and it was the same thing. Some ointment or liniment people put on aching joints . . . what was it called?

'Wendy. Did Jimmy use some strong smelly stuff, for arthritis?'

Wendy seemed surprised that I'd wander off on a tangent like this. Nonetheless she replied, 'Foul, sweet stinky stuff. Oil of Wintergreen. Methyl salicylate. It's an ester.'

'Of course. We made esters at school in Chemistry. But more importantly, Bill was wearing it when Robbie and I met him.'

Wendy was listening carefully. 'To me that's a silly mistake for him to make if he's impersonating his brother. I mean, it'd be a dead giveaway.'

'Yeah, but maybe he assumed no one would notice. Robbie can't smell a blessed thing and most people wouldn't notice. I just happen to have a big nose, I guess.'

'Makes sense. And your nose isn't big, by the way. I just recalled another thing — Jimmy used to be some sort of actor way back,' Wendy offered. 'And if this whole thing was planned — the

274

fire, the murder, taking over his brother's identity and wealth . . . '

We all fell silent with our own thoughts. Wendy had to sit. Killing your brother wasn't anything new — just ask Abel or Cain.

It was Heather who broke the silence.

'Mum, Miss Winters . . . Mr Jordan's brother must have been here a week ago if he was killed then. That means he flew here or came by ferry. Do they keep records of passengers? If they do then Dad can check, can't he?'

'That's brilliant thinking, Heather. You'll make a great detective,' Wendy said. 'I'll tell Dad.'

'Car rentals too, Mum.'

I was impressed with Heather's reasoning abilities and told her so. Jimmy's cleverly woven deception was unravelling, thread by thread.

Chris and Wendy returned. The coroner had said the body didn't have a front tooth missing whereas we all knew Jimmy did. The body was definitely not Jimmy's.

Chris had something else to say. 'I contacted Robbie. He was dealing with a small brush fire but he's on his way. He sounded exhausted, didn't believe me at first but he apparently felt Bill wasn't being honest with him yesterday when he said he found some medals by chance, but Robbie reckoned it was like he knew exactly where they were hidden.'

Over the following hour, feedback from Huonville police confirmed the dead man was in fact Bill. Dental records faxed from a Sydney dentist confirmed it.

Once Robbie arrived in his fire-fighting kit, Chris updated him. He listened attentively as he gulped down three glasses of water. The poor man looked dreadful. He'd been up since four that morning, responding to an emergency call-out.

'He certainly had me fooled,' Robbie said, sadly. 'But why kill your own brother, then masquerade as him?'

Considering 'Bill' was throwing cash

around in the pub and on expensive cars, it was evident to me. 'Money, Robbie. I believe that, after the fire, Jimmy went back to Sydney to fleece Bill's accounts and assets.'

'Yeah. Sounds logical, Debra. But he came back and met up with you and me. If anyone could see through his deception, it'd be me. I've known Jimmy almost all my life. He was a good man.'

Chris had the only logical answer. 'Arrogance. Jimmy thought his deception was foolproof and he wanted to test it with you. Also, it would have been suspicious if Bill never came to Tassie. If he hadn't slipped up with some facts that Bill should have known about, he would have gotten away with it, too. Pay his last respects in Tassie, then live the life of Riley back in Sydney as Bill, with no one the wiser,' Chris explained. 'Whatever the case, I'm getting changed then heading up to Hobart to arrest him at his hotel.' Wendy was concerned and told him so.

'Don't worry, love. I'll be with armed officers.'

He left us. It was out of our hands now. Bill — or Jimmy — would soon be under arrest.

My concerns were now for Robbie.

'The fires you were putting out. Were they set by this arsonist?'

He rubbed his eyes and gulped some more water. 'No, but the Hobart ones were, up on Mount Wellington. Mr Red Cap was spotted but got away.'

I took his hands in mine to give them a kiss. This time he didn't pull away. Instead he stared at me before beginning to sob.

'Oh, Debra! I still can't believe Jimmy could do what he's done.'

'People change, Robbie. You did — for the better — but Jimmy's done the opposite and what's more he planned it all out. He's not the man you were once friends with.'

Robbie sighed, wiping a still soot-covered hand over his eyes.

'You're right, Debra, absolutely right.

Jimmy was always a planner who didn't take chances. That part of him wouldn't have changed.' He gave a big sigh, and went on, 'I've been doing my own thinking. In between copying that arsonist by burning his house down and then turning up as Bill, he must have had a place somewhere to perfect this miracle transformation. There's no possibility he would have turned up at Bill's hotel looking like he was. They would have tossed him out on his ear.'

'Friends? Another house he owned? A caravan in the bush?' I was only trying to help.

Robbie sat back on a chair in the gallery, head in hands. When he raised his eyes again, he was staring at the black and white photo on the wall.

'I wonder . . . ' He rubbed the stubble on his chin, quietly musing for a moment. 'Debra, that's where Jimmy probably stayed.'

He lifted a frame down and put it on the table. I examined the photograph closely. Robbie, his mum and Wendy were outside an old weatherboard house.

'My father's place out west in the bush. That's where we'll find our answers.'

13

Robbie scowled as he told me, 'Our family home. Well, it was before Mum took us away from there. Jimmy used to go there before . . . before we left. Definitely not the happiest of places to grow up.'

'I'm surprised Wendy wants to display it, if it brings back bad memories,' I said. From what I'd heard, old man Sanderson was not nice to his family.

'That's precisely why we agreed to put it there. Despite the terrible times, we were all smiling. That shows our inner strength and that's not a bad thing to be reminded of every day.'

In a perverse way, it made sense.

'And if Jimmy was using it as a base?'

'We'll tell the police, Debra. He won't be there now. He'll be living it up as Bill. Once back at his hotel, he'll be arrested.'

I fingered the photograph on the table. Robbie was just a toddler there. What horrors had he already endured at the hands of his father? Was this why he was so distant as a man?

'I'll come with you. Going back there won't be easy but you'll have me by your side at least.'

He didn't argue.

Robbie's station wagon had firefighting gear in the back — blankets and two respirators with tanks, some axes too. As we stepped in, I asked him if he'd left a note about our destination. He told me no, but that he had the emergency radio if there were a problem. It was common-sense at the time. In retrospect, it was over-confidence. We had no idea what awaited us there.

It was so hot, Robbie had to turn off the air-conditioning after a few minutes as the car engine was overheating from the slow, bumpy drive. That meant opening the windows then sitting back as red dust and flies enveloped us. At least we could drink some cold water

I'd brought from the fridge.

The road narrowed to a pot-holed, rutted track. We were deep in the bush now. Robbie hadn't been back here since he'd left aged four. Once or twice, he got lost and had to retrace his route.

'Something on your mind, teach?' he asked.

I chose to be honest with him. 'I was just thinking how much I've come to trust you.' Images from my dream were haunting me even though I was wide awake.

'Trust? That's a strange word to use. I hoped we had more than that.'

He was disappointed, though without some definite commitment to wanting more from our relationship, I wasn't going to share my feelings with him . . . not yet.

Then he pointed. 'Tyre tracks. We've had a visitor out here.'

'Jimmy?'

'Possibly. We're pretty isolated. I believe the house is just around the next corner. I was only a nipper when we all left. Not before time.'

'What was the last straw that made your mum take you away?' I prompted as gently as I could.

'Rather not go into that right now, thanks, Debra. Jimmy's been though. That's his truck.'

Glancing at Robbie's face as he saw the homestead, I saw there was anger there as well as other dark emotions . . . fear? Yes, there was fear.

I rested my hand on his arm. 'Robbie. Your dad's gone. He can't hurt you now.'

The deep sadness of his whispered reply frightened me.

'He can, Debra. Every single bloody day.'

* * *

Once inside, it was evident that Jimmy had stayed here. There were discarded food packets scattered around the ancient kitchen. Flies and ants were all over the place. The bed had been slept in, new-ish sheets covering the old, stained mattress. The odour of rotting fruit completed the scene.

By contrast, there were things from years ago also there. A little steamroller next to its Matchbox cardboard container. A pink and white fluffy doggie and a box of Derwent pencils with a child's drawing of a fire-truck pinned to the boards behind. Someone had written *Bobby aged 4* in pen on the bottom.

I could understand why Jimmy had secreted himself here when his house was burned down, a hideaway to alter his appearance then return to Sydney as Bill to complete the transformation.

I turned to leave one of the two bedrooms but paused when I spied the object hanging behind the door. 'Robbie — you need to see this,' I called.

He came quickly. There was a red cap on the hook.

'No . . . no. Jimmy would never do that! Burning down his house to cover a murder is one thing, but all these bushfires . . . '

Robbie stood mutely, trying to fathom the warped mind of his one-time friend. He was devastated. Even I couldn't accept it. A firefighter turned fire-lighter?

For some bizarre reason, I recalled a book I'd read years before by Ray Bradbury — *Fahrenheit 451*, the temperature paper ignited. In the story the main character was a fireman in the future, but their job was not to put out fires, but to start them, to burn books in the dystopian future.

'Come on, Robbie. We have to radio this in to the police.'

He didn't move, lost in his own moment of trauma.

'Robbie — now.' Taking his limp hand, I literally dragged him from this house of horrors.

Thankfully he snapped out of his stupor once we got outside. He kept hold of my hand, though.

When we reached the car, he reached across to grab the microphone and flipped the power toggle switch. He pressed the button on the mike.

'Robbie to base. Over.'

Nothing.

It was then I noticed the end of the cord dangling on the floor.

Suspecting something, Robbie tried to start the engine but it refused to turn over.

'Damn. What's wrong with you, you dumb car?' he growled.

At the same time, the bushes parted ahead of us. Bill — or rather, Jimmy — stepped from the tinder-dry undergrowth, his hair in disarray from the winds. He had the Bakelite distributor cap from Robbie's engine in one hand and that rifle in the other.

Before we could do anything, he dropped the cap to the ground and crushed it with his foot — and then he levelled the menacing weapon at us.

'Hello, lovebirds. Long time no see.'

14

Robbie carefully moved around to put himself between Jimmy and me. 'Jimmy . . .' he began.

'Shut your mouth, Robbie. Get back inside, both of you. It's too hot out here. But I know for a fact it's going to get a bloody sight hotter. We're going to have us the grand-daddy of firestorms, right here in The Valley.'

It was an ominous statement but we had more pressing concerns. We moved in the direction indicated by the rifle Jimmy was waving. Any moment now, I expected him to shoot us in the back. Unbeknown to us, Bill's killer had more torturous plans for us.

We were herded back into the stinking lounge. Jimmy closed the makeshift door.

'It was you, girlie, wasn't it? You've got more brains than Robbie. Saw through my disguise, didn't you? Too bloody smart for your own good. What gave me away?'

Denial would have only inflamed him and that his trigger-finger.

'You got some things wrong. Where Raffles was, the time of your make-believe American conference, and another thing — Bill was wearing that same foul-smelling Oil of Wintergreen liniment that Jimmy did. That took me longer to realise. I'm guessing you escaped the police hunt for Bill.' That he was here and not in cuffs obviously meant he'd not been caught.

'When I rang the car rentals, they told me the police had been asking questions. I'd slipped him a twenty when I picked it up yesterday, just in case.'

I couldn't help myself. 'Your brother's money.'

'Bill doesn't need it any more,' he sneered.

'Even if you escape from Tassie, they'll still catch you.' I was desperate to delay the inevitable.

'Bill Jordan will disappear. I've

already cleared out his bank accounts.' He checked his expensive-looking watch. 'Better get a wriggle on. That firestorm I talked about — it won't be long 'til it arrives here, I reckon.'

We stared at him, aghast. He'd already lit it further up The Valley.

'This is not like a 1940s movie where the hero stops the villain just in time to prevent a catastrophe,' he gloated. 'The Valley and all its shops and homes will be one big inferno by morning. My little firestorm parting pressie.'

'Why?' shouted Robbie. 'You're a good man, Jimmy. You stop fires, not start them.'

'And for what? Volunteer fireman for all those years, putting my life on the line? Not one person said thanks. Not one. My wife walked out. Friends dumped me. It took a while to give up the drinking to make my plan pay off, though. Withdrawal, they call it. More like the worst sort of torture, but I did it. And when I was ready, I phoned Bill in Sydney. Told him I was sick so he'd come visit me, then I drugged him and killed him. Felt good. Always hated him and his success.'

That explained the smell of death when I first went to Jimmy's place. Bill's body was probably in the next room. It also explained why Jimmy fired the gun at the ceiling. He didn't want us discovering Bill's body before he'd had a chance to make him look like it was he himself that died in the fire.

'As for this,' he said, pulling padding from under his shirt then flinging it at me. 'Won't be needing that any more. Thought it would make me look different to Jimmy but it didn't work, did it?'

I didn't answer.

Jimmy checked his watch again. 'Right girlie. Tie him up.' He tossed some cord from the floor.

He stayed well back from us, his gun steady. Robbie wouldn't have a chance if he tried to jump him anyway, so I did as he asked.

'Fasten them tighter. I'm leaving you two here.' He checked the restraints then produced a knife.

'I'm not going to kill you, Robbie. The fire will. Have you told blondie here your secret yet? The one you've hidden for so long?'

Robbie squirmed and stared at the floor.

'Jimmy. Don't do this . . . . please.'

'Why don't we show her? Let's see if she's your one true love or if she'll despise you once she finds out the truth about you.'

With that he grabbed the hem of Robbie's shirt then cut and ripped it from his back with one strong pull. Robbie staggered. I gasped.

'Not a pretty sight, eh, girlie?'

The massive burns ran from Robbie's right shoulder across his back. So that was the reason he'd been afraid to become too close to me.

Jimmy was clearly hyped up, eager to explain what had happened.

'I saved little Robbie here when he was just four. I was visiting his dad, a young man eager to learn from an older builder. In spite of his father's nature, Robbie was happy but, for some reason that day, old man Sanderson was in a foul temper. He kicked over an old kerosene heater that was alight. The kero splashed all over Robbie, burning him. Should have heard the screams, girlie. Dreadful they were.'

I could imagine. I put my closed fist to my mouth, tears streaming from my eyes. All this time Robbie was turned away from me, ashamed of his disfigurement.

'Old man Sanderson just stood there shocked, doing nothing. So I did. Rolled him in a rug to smother the flames. Took him to hospital, him in agony and crying, his mum and sister trying to comfort him. Old man Sanderson. He drove away somewhere. Disappeared in case the cops came after him. The docs did what they could, but . . .'

I glanced at Robbie, my eyes drawn to the reddened, misshapen wounds.

'Ashamed of him, are you, girlie? Horrified? Guess what, Robbie. Another girlie who despises the real you, the monster.'

Switching my gaze to Robbie again, I saw him avoiding my eyes, saying nothing. It was time to show the two men who I really was.

'You got that completely wrong, Jimmy. You don't know Robbie, and you certainly don't understand me — or what love is.'

I touched the burned skin tenderly, Robbie shivered at my caress before straightening up, his head raised.

'These burns are a part of Robbie, but he's more of a man than you'll ever be, Jimmy. You — *you're* the only monster here.'

That shocked our assailant, at least for a moment. He called me some foul words before ordering me to turn around so he could bind my wrists.

Suddenly Robbie made his move.

Jimmy must have been expecting it. He sidestepped Robbie who crashed onto the floor head first. He moaned, groggy.

I cried out and, tried to bend down

to help. Jimmy wasn't having it. His patience had run out. Forcing me up against a wall he grabbed my hands and wrapped some old electrical cord around my wrists, knotting them close together. I'd never break those bonds.

'Being a gambling man, I'm giving you both a chance to escape. It'll have to be on foot as none of the vehicles will work. Mind you, running with your hands behind your backs? Don't fancy putting any of Bill's money on you surviving.'

He burst into laughter before pushing me to the floor beside Robbie.

'One last kiss, lovebirds. I'm predicting a hot time ahead for both of you. Ooroo!'

With those parting words, he closed the door behind him with a resounding bang. The sound of a car leaving from up the track was the death knell to our chances of survival. We were going to die — gruesomely.

Already I could taste smoke from whatever inexorable inferno Jimmy had unleashed.

'No! I'm not giving up!' I cried aloud. If I was going to die, I'd do it fighting. I tried desperately to struggle to my feet. I'd never realised how difficult it was if you couldn't use your hands for support. I managed it finally by inching my back up a door frame using my feet braced on the opposite side. It hurt like hell. Robbie was trying to do the same at another open door.

Once standing, I went to the kitchen, calling out, 'We need a knife to cut the bonds. I can't see anything.' The drawers clattered to the ground as I turned my back to grab the handles.

Robbie was still groggy, but he staggered in.

'Pen knife. In my pocket,' he said.

'Which one?'

'Trousers. Front right.' He twisted partially away from me as I backed up to him.

'Great,' I mumbled.

This was going to be difficult, fumbling around not able to see what I was doing. It would be potentially intimate and embarrassing too, given the position on the penknife. After a few unsuccessful attempts, he suggested simply tearing the pocket open.

The smoke from outside was now more noticeable. It was a difficult task. Whoever had sewn the blinking pocket on had done an excellent job!

At last it ripped and I could retrieve the knife.

Gingerly, I put it into Robbie's hands then turned to guide him opening it and cutting the restraints. I was confident that, even with things being so bleak, Robbie would find a way to save us.

He undid the cord around my wrists and I rubbed my hands to restore circulation.

'What next?' I asked him.

'My car.'

'We can't drive it, Robbie.'

'There's equipment in it we can use . . . I hope.'

We ran out and grabbed the blankets and breathing gear. It was then I recalled that most people in fires died from the smoke inhalation, or even from suffocation as the fire sucked all the oxygen from the air to use in combustion.

'What now?' Smoke was blanketing the western horizon, making the low sun very ominous. I grabbed the water bottles too, as Robbie scanned the surrounding area.

'There's nowhere, Debra. The house, the cars . . . it's all useless, and there's nowhere nearby that would protect us.'

'But you have to save us. My dreams. Wendy called them premonitions.'

Robbie put both arms on my shoulders, forcing me to look him in the eyes. 'Not now, Debra. We have to trust our minds, not fanciful wishes. I'm sorry.' He hugged me close to him. I wasn't ready to give up. This time, I forced him to listen.

'We have to hide,' I told him. 'In my dreams you told me to go down.'

Robbie suddenly pulled away. There was a glimmer of hope in his blue eyes.

'Down? Of course! But it's a slim

chance . . . Quick. Back in the house.'

Robbie appeared to have shaken off the effects of that blow to his head. He peered to the west and the billowing grey smoke covering the skies with an increasing haze. Red flames could be seen licking at the setting sun.

I followed him into the kitchen. For the first time, I noticed scorch marks on the floor — the place where he'd been burned.

'What are we searching for?'

He ignored me. I guessed he was intent on remembering a place from his childhood as he pushed furniture from one part of the floor to another.

'There. Under that cupboard. Help me shift it.'

As we did, a square trap-door became visible. There was a handle in the wooden floorboard. I was exasperated by his single-mindedness, not explaining anything to me. Then I understood. This had been a dreadful place to him. To come back here for the first time in decades was so traumatic, even now. As if realising I was with him and needed to be told, he explained, 'When you said 'down', I had a vision of this place under the floor, like an English cellar, I suppose. Lord knows why my father had it here in the middle of nowhere but I'm grateful he did. At least now. We can hide in there — it's metal.'

Straining those rippling muscles of his, he yanked the handle, rusty hinges groaning in protest. An opening emerged with another hatch underneath. It was metal. Once also open, we stood above a Stygian black hell hole. Would this be our safe hiding place — or our coffin?

Thinking we had a chance, my mind sifted through what we required if we went down there. The thought of it was terrifying. I spun around and opened a cupboard. Jimmy had left some stuff here. There was a torch and spare battery. Shining the light down, we could see how small it was — and that it was empty. It was about ten feet square and six feet high.

There was a musty smell. Surprisingly it was free of dirt and spider webs.

'Maybe he stored possum pelts down here?' I suggested. I'd heard about places like this from my grandad. The Tassie government had, for years, had a bounty on the marsupials that raided the orchards. Whatever the reason it was there, we didn't have much time before the house would be engulfed in a fiery inferno.

'Push the mattress down there, Debra. All the blankets you can find. And any food and water.'

'Trust a man to think of his stomach,' I joked in an attempt to stop me thinking we'd never come out of there alive.

'We might be down there for some time, Debra. This place is going to be a raging wildfire in minutes and it'll burn for hours. The whole place is one big pile of fuel.'

We could hear the crackling of dry vegetation burning. Flaming leaves drifted down outside the dirty windows

301

like red flakes of snow, blown ahead of the fire-front.

Together, we pushed and pulled what we needed through the opening which was barely wide enough for Robbie's shoulders. Taking my hands, he lowered me down.

The room was sweltering, though the box was thankfully cooler, being underground. One wooden wall of the house had caught alight as Robbie gingerly lowered himself in before closing the hatch — just as red-hot debris began to fall above us.

The hollow sounds of what might end up being our tomb reverberated around us as we stared upwards at the unseen conflagration enveloping Robbie's former family home.

The light from the torch was eerie, casting macabre shadows on the walls. There was a sign on one: *Aloysius Jones, Shipping PLC, Bristol.*

'A shipping container from Europe?' I asked.

Robbie nodded, and his larger shadow

did the same. 'It must have been sunk into the ground with the house built over it.'

There was a muffled explosion from up above.

'Petrol tank. Probably my car.'

It was a matter-of-fact comment. It must be unbelievable up there — like hell, I thought. I coughed. It was becoming hard to breathe.

Robbie passed me a mask with a tube attached.

'Watch me. Breathe slowly. These should see us through the worst.'

That word 'should' concerned me. Still, we had no choice.

Touching the ceiling with my fingertips, I drew them back quickly — it was too hot to touch — and now even the walls were warming up.

'Debra, just lie down, put the mask on and conserve your energy. Have a drink first,' Robbie advised. We made ourselves as comfortable as possible, leaning against blankets on the wall as we lay down.

There was another explosion, further away this time. Robbie fitted our masks and turned on the compressed air flow. Then he turned off the torch to conserve the batteries.

I snuggled up to him as we listened to the inferno above down here in the darkness together. The sounds of the fire above and falling supports echoed around our confined space as I gripped his hand.

Time passed and I must have dozed off. It was a good way to conserve oxygen. Being with Robbie was comforting but more than once, I felt him curl up by my side, whimpering like a frightened child. He'd been in here before, and part of that young boy's mind was reliving the horrors of whatever had happened then.

We would be safe, I realised. Could the same be said of The Valley and the people there? After all, what could possibly stop a firestorm as hungry as the one above, now heading for the town?

There wasn't a thing we could do to prevent the impending disaster. Robbie whimpered again. Thinking about the firestorm outside, I did too.

15

Sometime later, Robbie nudged me awake. He turned the torch on. 'Take your mask off, Debra. It's safe to breathe again.'

The air was hot and dry but OK. I sipped some water and passed the bottle to Robbie.

He lay back, staring at the ceiling.

'Fire. I hate it. We think we can tame it but we're kidding ourselves. I just pray that somehow they can stop this.'

We sat there, thinking and talking, all the time, part of us listening for changes to the noises from above. Checking my new battery watch, I pressed the button — the dial of red numbers told us it was ten thirty-one.

Suddenly, we became aware of a new noise, a rhythmic patter that slowly became louder and heavier. Distant rumbles of thunder joined in.

'Is that rain?' I dared to suggest.

'I reckon you might be right,' he answered, relief evident in the tone of his deep voice.

Rivulets of water soon appeared under the hatch, glistening on the walls as they ran down the walls to pool in the far corner.

It continued unabated for over an hour before gradually ceasing.

'Should we get out?' I said.

'Nowhere to go, Debra. Even if the fires are all out, we can't walk in the dark to anywhere where there's people. There's wild creatures out there.'

I laughed. 'Wild creatures?' Carnivores like the Tassie Devil weren't a threat to us. They were mainly scavengers in any case.

'There's a tiger out here. Or there was. I remember seeing it when I was young. My mum pointed it out and told me not to tell a soul.'

Surely there couldn't be a tiger out here. Where could it have come from? A zoo or a circus? Besides, it would be dead by now.

Robbie understood my incredulity. He explained, 'A Tasmanian Tiger. There was a family of them.'

'They've been extinct since 1930.'

'Trust me, Debra. They're still around. Is it any more difficult to believe than astrology or dreams predicting the future?'

I opened my mouth to protest before realising he was right. Mankind didn't understand all the mysteries of the world — far from it.

'I'm feeling cold all of a sudden,' I confessed.

Robbie wrapped a blanket around us, snuggling up to me. It felt good to be with him.

★ ★ ★

When we both woke, sunlight outlined the hatch's edge. We pushed it open and emerged to a scene of utter devastation, with water still dripping from the blackened trees. Even the outdoor dunny was in ruins. Some colourful rosellas swooped down from the pristine sky above, reminding me that life would survive, even in the midst of this scorched wasteland.

'Ready? It's a long walk, Debra.'

'Give me five minutes . . . call of nature.'

'Me too.'

Searching for some privacy in the surrounding wasteland, I kissed him, this time on the lips, before heading off.

When we met up again, I felt refreshed having splashed some pooled water on my face.

We began walking, holding hands like a couple in love. Maybe we were. The remnants of Robbie's shirt hung down, exposing his back as it swayed with his steps. Neither of us cared any more. My own torn blouse and jeans were evidence that we'd both experienced a terrible ordeal.

It was Monday morning, I realised.

So much for my first day as a Deputy Head.

Some dead animals were by the trackside. A wombat and a spotted quoll. It was a sad reminder of the ferocity of the massive blaze. Then we spied a car crashed into a tree. We approached it together before Robbie stopped me to go and investigate.

When he returned, he told me, 'Looks like Jimmy underestimated the speed of his firestorm, Debra. He must have crashed. Legs were pinned. He wouldn't have had a chance.'

He led me around the wreck so I didn't see too much. A kilometre or so further on, we paused to rest.

Just then, there was the noise of a car approaching from up ahead. Seconds later we saw it was a police car. Wendy jumped out as it pulled up, rushing to embrace us both. Chris was more reserved but still relieved to find us alive.

Robbie told him to call off the search for Jimmy as he was dead — for certain this time. We then explained all that had happened before Robbie asked how they'd known we were here.

'The photo of the old place was lying on the table. We put two and two together when we realised Debra wasn't staying the night with you, little brother,' Wendy explained.

I was grateful they'd found us. So were my feet.

'We did spend the night together — but not like you think,' I told her. 'We hid in some metal box under your old house.'

Wendy was surprised. 'That chamber of horrors? Our father used to put Robbie and me in there for hours on end. No reason. Mum and I went to clean it out after our so-called father died. Trying to purge those hateful memories.'

That explained Robbie's crying the night before. To be in there, surrounded by blackness, must have been agony for a child.

'You should have said,' I admonished him.

'It was bearable. And this time I had someone with me . . . you.'

It transpired that the torrential downpour had quenched all the fires before much damage was done. Schools

311

had been closed for the day, so I wasn't going to miss my first day as Deputy after all.

On the way back to town to be checked by the doctor, Wendy leaned over to me in the back seat of the police cruiser.

'Looks like you and my brother are OK, even now his secret is revealed. I'm glad. Venus will be, too — she's going to be around in both your lives for quite a long time! Just remember, Debra . . . fire and water signs.'

'Opposites attract, Wendy. Although I must admit those astrological readings you did all came true. The dream, too.'

Wendy laughed. 'Don't get carried away, Debra. Ask yourself. We base horoscopes on birth. Why then? Conception makes more sense, though it would be harder to work out! And Caesareans, premature births? Do they change your entire future because the stars differ?'

Just then, I saw a large animal in the green, unburned countryside. It was like a massive dog with stripes.

'A Tasmanian tiger!' I said excitedly,

pointing. Everyone looked out at the magical creature, a living Thylacine.

'There's nothing there, Debra. You must be hallucinating from your ordeal. Besides, Tassie tigers don't exist any more. They're extinct,' said Wendy, totally ignoring my claims.

'But . . . but you saw it. You must have. You all must have.' I was becoming exasperated.

Wendy took my hand. 'Debra. If you're going to be a part of The Valley, you must realise there's no such thing as a living Tasmanian tiger.'

Then she gave me a wink. I nodded, understanding at last.

'I don't suppose he has a name too, this imaginary Thylacine?' I asked, grinning.

'If he did, I reckon it would be Bruce. Theoretically, of course.'

I nodded. Bruce was a good name for a mythical creature that epitomised the mysteries of the Tassie bush. What a shame he was extinct. At least as far as the outside world was concerned.

16

Quite a few months have passed since the night of the fires, and I'm loving my role as Deputy Head of All Saints. The enrolment has increased so much, we've been able to take on a new teacher. She's young and enthusiastic, a real asset to our dedicated team.

As for Doris, she has a boyfriend too, a local farmer. She says she's settling down in Tassie, her wandering days behind her.

I'm still living with Chris, Wendy and Heather — who is developing into a talented, beautiful and mature young lady.

Robbie and I are taking things slowly. I've decided not to move in with him until we're married. If anything, our love has grown to the point where I regret every minute we're apart.

On the weekends I help him with the

renovation of his home. He's a brilliant builder and electrician and has a full order book to prove it.

When it comes to choosing colours, however, my lovely fiancé hasn't got a clue. He actually wanted to paint our new bedroom walls fire-engine red!

Wendy's my best friend, both at home and at school now. We share the chores and cooking. Life is good in every way — although I did have a major shock this morning as Wendy and I drove to school. Fortunately, Wendy was driving.

'I did your stars this morning, Debra. Smooth sailing from now on,' she told me.

'Happy ever after, eh? Sounds good to me,' I said, before sensing that something had been left unspoken.

'Definitely no surprises, Wendy?'

'Definitely . . . well almost definitely. The first set of twins will catch you and Robbie unawares . . . '

She grinned broadly.

'First set of . . . ?'

I took a deep breath then grinned back. I'd survived a firestorm, and I was a teacher. How hard could having my own children be?

We do hope that you have enjoyed reading this large print book.

Did you know that all of our titles are available for purchase?

We publish a wide range of high quality large print books including:
Romances, Mysteries, Classics
General Fiction
Non Fiction and Westerns

Special interest titles available in large print are:
The Little Oxford Dictionary
Music Book, Song Book
Hymn Book, Service Book

Also available from us courtesy of Oxford University Press:
Young Readers' Dictionary
(large print edition)
Young Readers' Thesaurus
(large print edition)

For further information or a free brochure, please contact us at:
Ulverscroft Large Print Books Ltd.,
The Green, Bradgate Road, Anstey,
Leicester, LE7 7FU, England.
Tel: (00 44) 0116 236 4325
Fax: (00 44) 0116 234 0205

Other titles in the
Linford Romance Library:

NEVER TO BE TOLD

Kate Finnemore

1967: Upon her death, Lucie Curtis's mother leaves behind a letter that sends her reeling — she was adopted when only a few days old. Soon Lucie is on her way to France to find the mother who gave birth to her during the war. But how can you find a woman who doesn't want to be found? And where does Lucie's adoptive cousin, investigative journalist Yannick, fit in? She is in danger of falling in love with him. However, does he want to help or hinder her in her search?

SURFING INTO DANGER

Ken Preston

All Eden wants to do is roam the coast surfing, at one with the waves and her board, winning enough in competitions to finance her nomadic lifestyle. But first the mysterious Finn, and then a disastrous leak from a recycling plant, scupper her plans. With surfing out of the question, Eden investigates. As the crisis deepens, who can she trust — and will she and her friends make it out alive from Max Charon's sinister plastics plant?

HIS DAUGHTER'S DUTY

Wendy Kremer

Upon her father's death, Lucinda Harting learns that she faces an impoverished future unless she agrees to marry Lord Laurence Ellesporte, who reveals that his father and hers had made the arrangement in order to amalgamate the two estates. For her sake and that of the servants, she accepts, though they live mostly separate lives. Until one day when shocking news reaches Lucinda's ears: Laurence has been arrested as a spy in France! Determined to secure his release, she heads to Rouen with Laurence's aunt Eliza, and a bold plan . . .

SUMMER OF WEDDINGS

Sarah Purdue

Claire loves her job as a teacher, but always looks forward to the long summer break when she can head out into the world in search of new adventures. However, this summer is different. This summer is full of weddings. When Claire meets Gabe, a handsome American in a black leather jacket and motorbike boots, on the way to her best friend Lorna's do, she wonders if this will be her most adventurous summer yet. Will the relationship end in heartache, or a whole new world of possibilities?

LOVE CHILD

Penny Oates

Knowing she was adopted, Lara was nevertheless happy with the parents who brought her up. But when she accidentally discovers her birth parents, she is catapulted into a life completely alien to her — and comes up against the insurmountable obstacle that is Dominic Leigh. She can't understand why he seems determined to keep her away from her father, or why he suspects her of wanting to cause trouble. She vows to overcome his interference, and in doing so, finds so much more than she had bargained for . . .